2024 Penelope Alonso – Copyright

All Rights Reserved. No part of this publication may be reproduced, distributed, or transmitted in any form or by any means, including photocopying, recording or other electronic or mechanical methods, without the prior written permission of the publisher, except in the case of brief quotations embodied in critical reviews and certain other noncommercial uses permitted by copyright law.

This is a work of fiction. Names, characters, businesses, places, events and incidents are either products of the creator/author's perspectives or imagination or used in a fictitious manner. Any resemblance to actual people/persons living or dead, or actual events, is purely coincidental.

ISBN: 9798326307620

CONTENTS

Yesterday
The Trail
Grandpop Tony
The Steps
Grandmom Philly
Celery Things
Running Away
The Hammering
Pop Pop
A Change in the Air
Where am I?
Alone With Everyone
The Rain Looks Different
Celebrated
My Mother
Experience
About Time
My Last Walk
Today
23 More Years

*This book is dedicated to my favorite person, **Sharon**. My beautiful mother, greatest friend, and champion of every step of **my walk**.*

Prologue

My grandmother told me of the time she looked out of her bedroom doorway late at night, peering into a coal-black hallway, in the weeks she lay ill as a child of not quite 11. She was fighting a kidney infection that brought with it delirium and high fevers.

It was at that time in her young life, she saw him.

Her older brother, who had died in childhood, waving at her.

The vision of him, his smile warm, his face joyous and his entire small body framed in a shimmering glow that poured over him like molten glass, even though he stood in a narrow, silent hallway of darkness in the South Philadelphia home in which they were both born.

She found this vision of him comforting, in those dark hours of the night, in her silent Mifflin Street home, which was cramped with her mother's parents, her younger sister, Marie, and several aunts and uncles, some of which had spouses in tow, all sharing three bedrooms, one bathroom and a small kitchen.

On this dark, eerily silent evening, seeing her brother's healthy smile, my grandmother felt as though he was bringing warmth to her. Her little body, cold and drained, felt renewed. He was, in her eyes, a light in her darkness. She told me about getting out of bed and walking down the narrow hall to meet him and, from there, going on a journey that took her far away from the isolation of her bed. She found herself walking with her brother on an Italian hillside of sunshine, worlds away from their shared childhood home.

Together, they explored a landscape of beach and ocean, peering into the succession of waves moving before them, all drenched in sunlight. She walked a path with her brother around the ruined church of St. Francis of Assisi, beyond houses with adorned facades, separated by narrow paths that dipped into the sea. They touched the brick walls of the Cattolica di Stilo as they walked one Calabrian hillside after the other, mapping a new place out of magic and time.

Little fingers clamped together, brother and sister on an impossible journey.

Stepping in the fresh, damp grass of an inviting hillside, leading to a house that seemed ready to welcome them, she sang songs with her brother – laughing in sunbeams that, to her, appeared to launch out of the small windows of the modest house on their path. She didn't know how long she was with her brother, but however long it was, it was a lifetime.

His name was Louis. My grandmother died over two decades ago, at the age of 79.

She told me this story of her walk with Louis **yesterday**.

Yesterday

I am not going to think about dying today.

Today is my birthday.

Today is only for breathing, for being in the place that makes my heart feel like it is home. As I stumbled toward the front door of the rustic Maine cabin my husband and I had rented so many summers as my kids grew up, I felt as though when I got to the porch, I would see them all—my three babies. My two daughters, my son, ready to hike, climb, swim, and explore. My husband.

Of course, the kids were coming later, with their families, in the case of my oldest, my son, and with friends, pets, and too many bags for spending too few days together in the case of my daughters. My children were no longer little ones who would run around the porch, dropping brownie crumbs everywhere and tripping over the frantic jumping of our golden retriever Sammie, who was no longer a part of this world, but who had watched my kids grow up and grow away for more than 16 years.

My children today are 32, 26 and 21.

One boy, two girls.

My life.

Soon to be together here, in this all too familiar cabin, with the bends and lifts of Acadia National Park's Cadillac Mountain in the cloud-drenched distance. This unremarkable old cabin, with its shuttered sides and timber frame that weathered nearly 120 years in the breezes off

Loon Lake — this little cabin, with pond water you must boil, a floor that creaks with almost every step and molasses-colored windows that ripple their memories in the sunlight.

This is a forever kind of place.

So many summers spent here. So many whispers of our happiest times filling the silent spots of the cabin. The year my son learned how to swim. The summer my youngest daughter finally let me splash with her in the ocean. The summer we celebrated my second born baby's acceptance to medical school. A million experiences, over time, one week every summer, the inherent familiarity of the Maine coast tying most of the best memories of my motherhood into a rustic bow.

Today is my birthday.

Today I turn 55.

I wasn't supposed to turn 55.

I wasn't sure I would ever make the trip to Maine again.

The truth is, this may be our last vacation in this cabin together, my children and me.

Cancer is a very fickle and frustrating friend.

I call my cancer a friend because I stopped fighting it months ago, resolved to take the journey with gratitude and strength – not bitterness, not despair and not devoid of hope. At the same time, I grew tired. Weak with worry, drained from appointments, procedures, tests, and sleepless nights. Dwelling on finances, flaking away with my inability to keep pace with the demands of my job, and my inability to do without working. Cancer is an extremely inconvenient and depleting friend. The kind of friend that wears us out – high maintenance. We all have them, those friends in our lives who are sometimes too demanding, a little too dramatic, maybe even a trace bit narcissistic. We all have those friends who can be gloriously overwhelming, yet inherently innocent, unaware of the energy they take.

This is the kind of friend Cancer can be. Pulling at you when you are weak. Forgetting your birthday. Laying all its woes and energy on you, expecting you to carry it while it pushes down your resolve to carry yourself. I'm not saying it's a terrible friend. I mean, I must thank Cancer for bringing me to new depths of appreciation and gratitude for every moment of my life. I must recognize it as being the single most impactful presence in my life in terms of strengthening me to face my mortality – to embrace the passing of my days with an enthusiasm, even a wonderous joy, that at times is nearly addictive. High-maintenance friends can give so much, and take so much, at the same time.

Today, though, I'm not letting Cancer take a thing from me. I'm claiming myself today.

Sorry, Cancer, I'm not taking your energy today, or thinking about your issues, or worrying about your longevity. I don't have time for a quick lunch at your discretion, followed by a quicker rush to vomit the quick lunch even quicker. Not today, my friend. Today is not yours. Lovingly, go fuck off a bit, we'll catch up soon enough – you'll be fine without me for a day.

It's been more than six years since we all made it here again, all together, each of us, from our respective launch points, driving to the serenity that always welcomed our family to the fresh air and nurturing peace that was our summer family paradise *Downeast*.

My oldest, my son, Michael, a mechanical engineer, now on his way, with his wife, Ashley, a dedicated and nurturing third-grade teacher, and their daughter, my only little grandchild, so far, my sweet little Julia, turning all of three years next month. Michael is driving up from Bryn Mawr, Pennsylvania. My daughter, Victoria, a neurology resident, is heading up to Maine from Massachusetts, with my youngest, Liz, freshly graduated from college. It's a trip each of my children know well, growing up making the haul from New Jersey to the Kittery and, as years went forward, Boothbay Harbor and later the Bar Harbor regions of Maine, for summer vacations over more than 18 years of tradition.

For this trip up, I drove alone.

I wanted to get to the house first and have a chance to collect my thoughts before the cabin came alive with commotion. The drive gave me time to think, to talk to my high-maintenance friend, to listen to my favorite podcasts about mindfulness and nutrition, about living with grief and loss – about reconnecting with myself. All topics ideal for a middle-aged mother, arguably young widow, and increasingly negligent cancer warrior. The long drive allowed me to revisit some of my favorite Jane Austen places on audiobooks that kept me focused on the road to Maine, and lost exploring the sands and cliffsides of Sanditon, and the rolling hillsides of Derbyshire.

My husband would have loved this trip.

Of course, with him, there would be no in-depth podcasts encouraging mindfulness and self-exploration, and absolutely no audio accounts of the exploits of Elinor Dashwood, Charlotte Heywood or even the fierce Elizabeth Bennet. Our drive up, with windows down and hours of meaningless conversation way up, would be fueled by my husband's playlist which pumped everything from AC/DC to INXS. He would have loved the pilgrimage up to Maine, settling in at this very cabin and waiting for the kids to join us.

Maine was where he *always* wanted to be. He won't be with us on this Maine getaway, at least not in body, but, in spirit, he'll find a way. He's the reason we are all Maine lovers in the first place. It was his idea to explore Maine when he and I were staying a few days in Worcester, Massachusetts, for a business conference I attended when we were newlyweds. Just two young and in love people who ridiculously thought the age of 30 was pushing AARP entitlement.

One night, after I finished my conference duties, he realized we were, as he put it, *right near* Maine, and so we got in the car and drove. About 90 minutes later we were in Kittery, Maine, the southernmost town in the state. Neither of us had ever been as far north as Maine. It was our own little mission of discovery. We explored as much as we could considering we rolled into Kittery at nearly 10 p.m. on a random Thursday, but we saw enough.

Kittery led us through the coastal historic wonder of York, Maine, and there, in the early hours of the random Friday morning that followed the random Thursday evening, we discovered along Route 1 remnants of the earliest of English settlements in the nation – with houses and buildings reaching back hundreds of years. York was founded in 1652 and, somehow, here it was, gloriously waiting for us to discover it. Our unplanned exploration of a state neither of us had ever visited culminated with our discovery of the hauntingly captivating Nubble Lighthouse, situated on a nub of rocky Maine coast that had served as a beacon for ships since 1879.

It was one night.

One tank of gas.

One little lighthouse.

One random Thursday exploration turned into our family's happiest summer vacations in a place that always felt like home. As time went on, and toddlers turned to young adults, our explorations continued – always looking for that one pond, or lake, or lighthouse we had yet to meet. We stayed in York. We stayed in Boothbay Harbor. Then, as we fell in love with Acadia National Park in the Bar Harbor region of the state, our rental cabins graduated to other coastal towns. We landed on our favorite cabin after the first summers in Maine, and it became our favorite spot – this warm, rustic cabin with just enough space to feel free, and Loon Lake practically off its sprawling wooden deck.

I'm so grateful we took that random Thursday night exploration.

My husband was always the explorer.

Of course, like so many of us who are married long enough to feel like an old couple, but not long enough to truly grow old together, I thought we had more time. Time to find more lakes and lighthouses. He wanted to explore Nova Scotia, just a ferry ride from Bar Harbor, Maine, to

Yarmouth, Nova Scotia. Somehow, we never fit the ferry into our summers with the kids. At some point, we figured Nova Scotia would be our exploration later, when the Maine trek was just us again, two crazy old kids, exploring new places.

It's funny how *later* carries such an empty position of power.

See you *later*.

What are you doing *later*.

We'll plan for it *later*.

We'll work it out *later*.

Later can go fuck itself.

I know, that sounds dramatic, if not overtly crude, but *later* can, in most instances, be very hollow. How much appreciation should I really show *later*? Equal parts promise and hope and disappointment and regret, *later* is a word that, in its overuse, has found a liberty that takes too much for granted, puts us all too at ease and, at the same time, promises to change its behavior.

And now, not *later*, here I am, facing my mortality at 54.

Wait, today is my birthday.

Facing my mortality – at 55.

I wasn't planning on facing my husband's mortality three years ago. I certainly wasn't planning on facing my own this soon after he left us. If I'm being honest with myself, I wasn't planning on most of what I was living right now. Almost no part of my life, right now, was what I thought was coming *later*.

Still, this trip—this escape to this little cabin—this rustic, yet impossibly comfortable dwelling enveloped by the woods of Maine, a few fast steps from the calming ripples of Loon Lake.

This I did plan.

I wanted us all to be right here – together, for perhaps the last time.

Making my way into the cabin, I let out a breath that felt as though it pushed out everything bad in my life, everything bad in my body, everything filling my mind—all of it, every push of air from my lungs, all out, all released. With the next breath, bringing in a new batch of air, I felt good. Really good. Better than I should. I unpacked my bags, clothes, groceries and, within two hours, as the morning ticked toward the start of afternoon, I made my decision.

My kids would not arrive until the very late this evening.

I had the entire day to myself.

And as excited as I was to see them – all of them – I was almost equally elated to have a day alone in my favorite place. Just me. Just today. Just right now. The drive here took me two days, stopping along the way to see sights in Connecticut, and so my arrival, days in the making, was an arrival I fully and energetically embraced.

Maine welcomed me with some of my favorite weather. The day was a painting of vivid blue sky with massive clouds of the purest white. It was a beautiful day that only Maine could paint for me. I found myself feeling oddly optimistic. Everyone I loved the most in this world was on their way to see me, in the place that I loved the most. As I stood looking at the sky, wondering how far my eyes really could see into the clouds that towered above, a thought came over me like a whisper that floated over the boards of the porch, through the rippling molasses-ribboned windows and over my shoulders sending tingles through my body.

Why don't you take a walk?

I would take myself to Acadia National Park, and head to one of the many trails that my husband and I had walked with our kids during the many summer vacations we made Downeast our home. I had never gone alone. Walked alone. But I knew it was what I wanted to do most on this day. So, I set out, my black canvas backpack filled with water bottles, crackers and cheese and orange juice, and of course, my fully charged mobile phone—which I refused to look at for the rest of the day. I was only going to walk the trails of Acadia National Park, my favorite trails, no phone, no music, no texting, no picture taking, no thinking. No great explorations. Just easy trails. Familiar trails. A walk with two gifts Maine was so good in sharing: Nature and Peace.

Just me.

Just the trail.

I got in my car, drove to Acadia National Park, left my car in a prime parking spot at Bubble Pond, and could not believe the tranquility that welcomed me. I was the only car in the parking lot. That *never* happens during the rush of August tourism, especially on a beautiful day like today. As

I stepped out of the car, a breeze tossed my hair over my eyes, and it felt freeing. Warm and soft, moving the strands of my hair like tiny paint brushes dancing over my forehead, eyebrows, and eyelids. I stood there, letting the breeze paint its warmth over my face. This felt like a homecoming. My own private welcome back. Flinging my backpack over my right shoulder, I breathed deep the warm August air and began to make my footprints in the gravel and dirt that twisted away from Bubble Pond and into the wooded wonders of the Maine trail before me.

I love this day.

It's my birthday.

Right now, not *later*.

The Trail

The trail was unusually empty, which fit nicely with my hope for a sublime experience. When you live with cancer, you look for sublime experiences. You want normal days, even boring days, anything to remove the sense of urgency cancer brings.

The trail felt wonderful crunching under my sneakers.

The occasional biker or random passerby excluded, it was mostly me and the ground beneath my feet. Soft and consistent, the mellow, temperate August breeze seemed to walk with me, and I appreciated its company. The medications I took to stave off the high-maintenance friend poisoning my body could sometimes make me feel overheated, nauseated, and way too fragile, but the kindly breeze rising off Bubble Pond supported me with the brushing touch of a good-natured friend, lending just the right amount of silent support and aware companionship.

The early steps of the trail were blissfully unremarkable.

The crunching, crackling of sun-dried layers of leaves and withy twigs scattered by little paws and claws of squirrels and chipmunks were music to my ears as I walked straight down the middle of the trail. The dirt felt cool under my sneakers as I crunched and crackled my way over the grains that dusted the topsoil. Entertaining my imagination were thick markings made by bike treads, sneaker and boot designs etched into the grit and pebbles, and crisp engravements of stroller wheels propelled over the gravel by young mothers and fathers introducing their babies to the delicate artistry of Maine's natural grace.

I loved the feeling of the sun, the warm thickness of its sunbeams poking through the treetops and falling on my cheeks, shoulders, and arms. On the trail not 15 minutes I soon felt 20 years younger – free of worry, free of illness. A day without the drain of my high-maintenance friend.

A day not to think about *later*.

I was thinking what a good idea this walk was when I heard it. At first, barely perceivable, a hint of a sound, faint as it rode the welcoming August air around me. A tingling, jingling sound so subtle it drifted over the trees and bushes and seemed to tingle and jingle around me.

Why is this sound so familiar?

Stopping to try to locate its source, I realized that, still, and remarkably, no one was around me. How is it that I was completely alone on this popular trail, during the height of the final weeks of tourism in this beautiful place. Where was everybody? The ting, ting, tingling sound consistently rode the August air, lifting and falling with the changing ripples of the summer breeze that swirled and whooshed around me. Ting, ting, ting. Ting, ting, tingling, tingling, ting, ting. The sound played crisply in my ears, throughout my body, as if the tone of the sound resonated with a tone within myself that I had not heard for a long time. Ting, ting, ting. Ting, tingling, ting.

Ting, ting, ting.

My thoughts drifted to Sammie. Our golden retriever. She joined us as a puppy when my youngest daughter was only two. Sammie grew up with my kids, was one of my kids and her death at age 16 several years ago, still left a sinking hollow in my heart. Her pink and purple woven collar would make the lightest tingling sound as she puttered through the house, yard, or even this very Maine trail I was on right now, hearing this tingling, ting, tingling, ting around me.

Where is everybody?

Ting, ting, ting.

Ting, ting, ting.

Fading in and out of rooms, up and down the stairs, anywhere she put a paw. It was this tingling that I heard, this jingling bell tingling, ting, ting, tingling, coming from what seemed every direction on this sun-soaked trail.

Ting, ting, ting,

Ting, tingling, ting.

This doesn't make sense.

Someone must have the same kind of collar on their dog – somewhere nearby on the trail. I took in a deep breath, almost in honor of Sammie. When my daughter Victoria was only six, she came with me to pick up Sammie. This was the dog she picked out of all the other barking, jumping dogs waiting for a forever home at our nearby animal orphanage. Sammie was the one that jumped with Victoria, ran in the animal orphanage's yard with Victoria, and seemed overjoyed to see my Victoria from the first few minutes the two locked eyes.

With my son busy at basketball practice, and my youngest daughter barely advanced into toddlerhood, it was Victoria who would play the biggest role of welcoming Sammie into our family the day we brought Sammie home. The memory of watching Victoria, with her honey blonde waves, brilliant blue eyes and gleeful smile running around the yard with Sammie on Sammie's first afternoon with us would forever play in my heart. Sammie would complete our family, growing with Victoria and our little family. And Sammie did, for just over 16 years, and a few days, until she could grow with us no more.

Where is everybody?

The tingling no longer drifted through the trees. As silence took over the trail, I saw her. The dog, a golden retriever that looked exactly like Sammie in her prime, sat motionless a few feet down the trail, the now, somehow, very soberingly silenced stretch of dirt.

All sounds stopped. The crisp and busy pattering of the forest animals. The chirpings of the birds. The gentle tossing of leaves in the passing breeze. The audible swing and sway of the wooded canopy.

The ting, ting, *tingling*.

It all stopped.

And while I knew it could *not* be her, I felt, at the very same time, that it could only be *her*. I called out, despite knowing it would likely result in an embarrassing encounter with whoever the owner of this golden retriever was and, before I could stop myself, my voice commanded the silence to open its secrets.

"Sammie?" I yelled forward as I knelt on both knees and patted the dirt before me. "Sammie, is that you? Here girl, here girl, Sammie? Sammie?" The dog's tail whipped wildly left and right with excitement as it perked up, got on all fours, and danced a bit in place. Its motion was fueled, almost frenzied, as if it had been sitting patiently for the command to move.

As the dog hopped and pattered in place, the ting, ting, tingling started up and then, with no provocation, the golden dog, with fur almost glowingly brilliant, as if painted with sunbeams, turned, and bounced away, straight and boldly leaping into the wooded thick off the side of the trail and, with a catapulting push into the trees, the dog was gone.

I got to my feet, feeling dizzy from the motion, but determined to spot that dog.

When I got to where the dog had veered off the trail, I noticed a tiny, almost imperceptible path. It may have at one time been a trail that shot off from the one I was on, the larger and typically vigorously traveled trail. This little path, though, seemed accessible and, as I looked forward, I could see it spun its way into the trees and bushes, carving its way in the direction of Bubble Pond – where the trail started. The dog must have run off in this direction.

I stepped forward.

As I looked down the path, covered in specks of sun, I could not see the dog. I heard it though, the tingle, tingle, tingle of the collar that our Sammie, or this Sammie substitute, had around its sun-soaked, furiously golden fur. Ting, ting, ting. Ting, ting, ting. As I walked, the tingling sound grew faint and as I turned a small bend where the trees almost closed me in, making my way down this narrow, yet visible path, I saw him.

An older man, only a few steps away from me.

He was standing, facing down the trickling remnant of the path ahead of me. I could see he was peeling an almost oversized, radiantly ripe red apple with a small pocketknife, artfully and patiently streaming the red peel into a brilliantly concise, decorative ribbon that hung over his wrist and stretched toward the dirt, dripping the sweetness of the apple it devotedly encased only seconds earlier.

I stopped.

I didn't feel threatened, just a few steps behind me sat the larger, more popular trail and on it there were *almost* always walkers, bikers, avid bird watchers or joggers at any given time - it was early in the day. Surely, the trail would soon be filled with couples, families, people of all ages, enjoying the beauty of Acadia National Park.

The solitude I experienced earlier certainly would not continue. It must have been an odd lapse in trail traffic, nothing more, nothing less.

People were *everywhere*.

I was fine.

I watched the old man break the apple peel away and as it hit the dirt, still gloriously as one ribbon, he carved off a piece of the apple, used the knife edge to bring it to his mouth and started chewing. The ripeness of the apple was almost astonishing. He spit a little as he chewed the apple, the sunlight catching the small and ample bursts of what I assumed was sweetened moisture spraying from his mouth. He took more bites of the apple, its nectarous juices obviously tasteful to the old man, who continued to chew with a savory appreciation, as if he had not tasted an apple in a long, long time. With each bite, the gratifying sweetness of the apple seemed to invigorate the old man, who continued to spit and chew, spray and swallow, the divines of this particularly delectable apple, until every edible component of the apple was absorbed. He tossed the core into the bushes and gave the red ribbon at his feet a little kick forward.

I didn't move.

This old man was familiar.

His hair was speckled with mostly gray, but small brownish, blackish whisps peppered about his head and stopped at the nape of his neck and temples. His glasses were thick. I could see from the moment his head turned to the side slightly, his profile was strong. His shirt was a green that I knew, a soggy olive-toned, buttoned cotton shirt, tucked into almost maroon pants. The old man had his sleeves rolled up exposing his very tanned arms and as I watched him, still giving a slight kick to the red ribbon of apple that decorated the dirt before his shoes, I knew who he reminded me of, almost eerily.

His small frame. His strong profile. His leaning to one side, as if one leg were stronger than the other. That tanned skin. His soft waves of salt-and-pepper hair. That tiny knife that I now watched him fold and tuck away in his pant pocket.

The way he wiped his wet mouth with the back of his tanned right hand, fingers outstretched.

He started to laugh. Still not looking at me - *did he know I was looking at him* – his laugh shook his frame. His laugh was one of deep amusement, as if the funniest joke in the world were told and he was the only one to hear it, causing him to laugh so hard he began to cough and spit a little as his laughter ran away from him, too big, too robust for his small frame to contain.

My memory flashed back to a brisk late October afternoon at the New Jersey home where I grew up, and where he lived in his final years. To the backyard, where my grandfather and I busily bagged crisp, dried fallen leaves, which I, all of age six or seven, gingerly placed on a worn and tattered lawn tarp. At one point, he stopped me, watching me load the leaves with the care of transporting porcelain, he began to laugh. And laugh. And laugh. When he laughed to a point arguably of ridicule, he would spit while he laughed, sprays of ridicule in droplet form.

I was not amused.

Even as a little girl, when I could see I was the source of his amusement, I resented it. Greatly. I remember looking at him, puzzled. I thought I was doing a good job. Wasn't I moving the leaves nicely enough? Was there no structure to this task? Clearly, I was mistaken, as his almost mocking laughter practically choked him, as I stood directly in front of him, proudly clutching my handful of fallen leaves, feeling my cheeks rush with red over his glee at my expense.

Standing on this path, this confined, narrow piping of sullen dirt, I felt like that little girl again – standing there, holding my dried leaves, wondering what's going on and why he's so amused.

I wanted to move, but I could not.

I just looked at him.

And as he began to turn his thin body toward mine, his laugh now quieting to a hushed lull of almost exhausted patience, his eyes followed the dirt trail, up and up, until they met my own and in that moment I had no longer any doubt of who this old man was, impossible or not.

"Whaddaya doin?" he said, looking over at me and pointing to my sneakers. "You walkin in them; how much didja pay for them - they don't look too good." He smiled, and winked at me, and with a turn of his shoulder to face the trail ahead, gestured for me to join him. The quick movement of his left hand, rapid circular motions by his side, as if moving the air would pull me to his side with each wrist turn. After a few turns of his wrist, he stopped.

I did not move. I felt defiant, yet inexplicably so. I felt like a child again, small, yet purposeful. That little girl, with whisps of brown hair down her shoulders, holding handfuls of delicate dried leaves, refusing to move, trying to figure out my circumstances.

The old man gestured again.

"Listen," I told the old man, outstretching my left hand and placing it into the air as if to stop something coming straight at me. "Listen, this all feels very…very strange. I, I don't know you. We don't know each other. I mean, it's not possible. This…this is not possible. You are not possible. None of this is possible. None of this is possible. None of this is possible."

I found myself repeating my words, as if to wake myself, or remove him from my sight.

He remained.

Even more frustrating for me, he smiled.

"I don't know you? I don't know ... *you*? I knew you, before you knew you. When you were not anything, I knew you. Before you could talk, I knew you. Before you were named, I knew you. And you know me, *Penny*," he said. "We have a way to go and if we don't get started right now, you will not be able to finish - you're going to miss a lot, and I don't want you missin anything. Not nothin. Not today. Besides, it's your birthday, even more important we don't waste time, let's move."

He called me Penny.

My given name, the name my parents picked for me, was Marielle Elaine, a name wrapped in homage to generations of aunts and grandmothers, but my Dad's father, my Grandpop Tony, he called me *Penny*.

It started from my birth.

Grandpop Tony saved hundreds and hundreds of pennies to buy me one of my first tiny toys, so, in a nod to the diligence of his thrifty ways, and his excitement over the luck of becoming a grandfather, the name *Penny* spoke to him. Loudly. As it happened, the name Bonnie also spoke to him, because, for reasons I don't know, he liked the look of women in bonnets. *Penny* or Bonnie? Bonnie or *Penny*? Ultimately, he settled on *Penny*, and once that decision was made, it was a matter of not much time at all until every family member, on both sides of my family, called me *Penny* – my mother being the last holdout in the quest to retain some connection for me to my given name.

She would not be successful in her endeavor. Ultimately, and with little choice, my mother also embraced, or rather willfully accepted, *Penny*, and, with her acceptance, the renaming takeover, orchestrated perhaps innocently enough by my Grandpop Tony, was over.

Penny was the champion.

Everyone who knew me from birth or blood knew me as *Penny*. Aunts, uncles, first cousins, second cousins, third cousins twice removed, longtime neighbors, friends of my parents and grandparents – anyone who knew me through a connection to family, knew me only as *Penny*.

I had many relatives who thought my given name was Penelope.

It was not. Still, *Marielle Elaine* became two words strung together for school or, later in life, work or any friends and relationships I created on my own, separate from life as *Penny*. One person. Two names. One built on generational ties, the other bestowed by little more than a whim. Anyone who grows up with a nickname knows the deal.

Of course, with the passing of time, and generations turning over in my family as years tumbled into decades, the number of people calling me *Penny* began to equal the number of people calling me Marielle. It occurred to me, somewhere around the age of 40 or so, that, one day, Marielle would be the winner of the name game. Marielle would be the name I heard the most, in my daily life – eventually far outpacing the nickname that connected me to a coin, albeit lovingly so.

Marielle Elaine was playing the long game.

"Penny," the old man called to me. "I'm glad you are here. I, I don't believe this all too, but here we are, Penny, here we are."

Grandpop Tony died when I was just staring fourth grade, in fact, he died the first day of school that September. His cause of death was stomach cancer, which spread to his liver. He was given six months to live when his initial diagnosis was told to him by the best doctors in Philadelphia and, two years after that, he finally succumbed. Grandpop Tony's high-maintenance friend was either generous for giving him more time than he thought was possible, or cruelly self-sacrificing in giving him just enough time to fully comprehend his decline.

The last time I spoke with him was on the phone, he was in his hospital bed, soon to be his death bed, and I was at my Aunt Elvira's house on Mifflin Street in South Philadelphia. The Mifflin Street house was at the corner of Ninth and Mifflin streets, with a grand elementary school commanding the adjacent city block and tiny corner stores that sold water ice, candy, Italian rolls of all shapes, fresh fruits, meats, and cheeses. Mifflin Street was filled with people who were either born in Italy, just arrived from Italy, were visiting from Italy, or were first-generation Italian Americans sending letters, money and pictures back to parents and grandparents still living in Italy.

Everyone on Mifflin Street was somehow identified by where in Italy they originated.

Naples or Sicily, Florence or Sorrento, or, like both sides of my father's family, Calabria, the southern Italian peninsula that was the place where it is said Pythagoras, one of the fathers of Western philosophy, began to share his thoughts. Calabria, with its population of Greek and Italian mixed together in person, language, and culture, once the home of the Bruttii, ancient peoples of southwestern Italy first known to occupy the *'toe of the boot'* of the land of porcini mushrooms and olive oil.

The Bruttii commanded Calabria during the Third Century. My father's family did a command of their own on Mifflin Street, where both Grandpop Tony and Grandmom Philly were firmly woven into the tapestry that was Italy transported to the mouth of the Delaware River.

There were only two trees on Mifflin Street by the time my childhood hit the slice of little Italy that was the neighborhood that reared my grandparents, and my father. The Mifflin Street house was packed with people, originally purchased by my Grandmom Philly's grandparents, it was the site of births, funerals, weddings, and every holiday in between until, eventually, the house came under the ownership of my Aunt Elvira.

During my Grandpop Tony's final days, Aunt Elvira would watch my younger brother and me when my Grandmom Philly could not, as my mother and father worked long days. With Grandpop dying in the hospital, Grandmom Philly stayed by his side - leaving Aunt Elvira on weeks of babysitting duty. It would be my Aunt Elvira who would hand me the receiver of her classic black phone, giving me the tool through which to hear my grandfather's voice for the last time.

The last time I heard my Grandpop Tony's voice was not a happy memory.

My Aunt Elvira called the hospital to check on him and decided to put my brother and I on the phone. Grandpop Tony began coughing violently, after first saying a few words to my brother, and, listening intently, I could hear the rushing cough that overtook his body, causing him to hang up the phone without speaking to me. The receiver of the phone banged and banged until I guess he found its resting spot, or perhaps his nurse, or one of his brothers, or even my Grandmom Philly, hung it up. I remember the sound of him, as he struggled to catch his breath in those loud and frantic seconds, chopped silent by the phone receiver mercifully hitting its perch.

I had never heard anything so violently crippling. I thought something must be very wrong with Grandpop Tony.

I was right.

That would be the last exchange I had with him.

Until now.

"I don't feel very well all of a sudden," I told him, stretching my hands out in front of me, fingers spread, as if to put a stop to whatever might come next. "I'm on a lot of medication, I'm not comfortable with this, whatever is happening here, I'm not sure if any of this is right, or even real – I'm walking away now." As I spoke to the old man, I gestured both of my hands and outstretched fingers, as if to gesture him away, or perhaps, somehow wave away what was increasingly becoming more difficult to accept as real.

"Penny, I know you are on lots of pills, and you're doing what the doctors are telling you, I know, I know better than anybody the things you think about, but it's gonna be alright. "I promise you, you are gonna see, you are gonna be fine, this ain't the end of you, you're not going away, not yet, not now," he told me.

He reached out again for me to take the four or five paces I needed to be by his side.

What to do?

Convinced this was a hallucination, or a dream - *maybe I passed out on the bigger trail, and all of this is a glimpse of the afterlife, or maybe I am just shockingly dehydrated* - I took the few steps I needed to be next to him, this old man, this familiar old man that was not even 15 years older than I was on this very strange birthday.

This familiar old man, who calls me *Penny* and looks and sounds like my Grandpop Tony.

This small man, exercising a patience that my Grandpop Tony was not known to possess. This olive-skinned, smiling old man, with all the time in the world for me. I stood almost touching his shoulder, separated only by a slight breeze.

He smiled.

I smiled.

And we began to walk.

As we took our first steps forward, side by side, I began to feel at ease.

Grandpop Tony

When my kids were little, every summer, when we could afford to do so, my husband and I brought them to Maine for a week. We would stay in Deer Isle, or Blue Hill, Gouldsboro, or Seal Harbor. Sometimes we stayed in the Echo Lake region as near to Acadia National Park as possible. We could never afford to stay in Bar Harbor. There were some summers when the drive to Acadia was well over an hour from our rental house, and others when getting to the beauty of Bubble Pond, Cadillac Mountain and the trails of Acadia took minutes. There was one summer rental we all loved best. This was the one we went to the most summers. The one everyone built their greatest memories around.

The cabin I secured for this very trip.

That cabin seemed so far away right now.

As I took steps in silence next to my grandfather, who had been dead for over 40 years, I thought about all the rental cabins that made Maine home to my family over the years, and how my grandfather never set foot in Maine during his 68 years on earth. In what I can only describe as a stupor, or maybe reasonable shock, my walk with Grandpop Tony started with a kind of guarded apprehension, a curious firing of random memories, logical assumptions, and rapid self-preservation reminders.

I'm walking with my dead grandfather.

Where is everyone, walkers, hikers, why is there no one else here? What if I die right now? Am I hallucinating?

How far away did I park? Maybe I passed out back at the beginning of the trail. I did forget to take my medicine on time this morning, I wonder if ...

"You need to take it easy," he said to me, still walking, breaking into laughter as he finished his thought. "You're gonna drive yourself bananas, nobody needs to be bananas today."

My Grandpop Tony was funny.

Not so much *intentionally*.

He was born in 1910 in South Philadelphia to Italian immigrants who never spoke a hint of English and lived almost his entire life within the span of 14 city blocks, immersed in the Italian American neighborhood of brick rowhouses that was his world. He had three sisters. Four brothers. And one adopted brother who may have been the victim of a mob hit - but the family never talked about it and so, that brother's true story is lost to the lore of family whispers.

He was born on McKean Street on the third floor of a house that saw the birth of almost all his siblings. During his birth, the midwife, who I imagine was doing the best she could, grabbed onto his legs too hard and, in doing so, crippled one of his legs permanently. I don't really know what exactly happened during his birth to give him the pronounced limp that became distinctly and prominently his, but, whatever the midwife did, or didn't do, or whatever happened on that sticky, sweltering late June evening that announced his birth, he would never walk smoothly.

He would always dip when he walked. Still, he was resilient, if not irrepressible, despite his burdensome amble. He was also what we would lovingly call, a *character*.

He could fix most of the problems your car might be giving you with wet wads of painstakingly chewed bubble gum, yards of duct tape, Valvoline, and a wrench.

If you walked into a store with him and he was wearing his raincoat, be sure he was walking out with candy bars for you - in his coat pockets. You'll have no memory of him paying for them.

Convinced he could negotiate the best deal for my father's first car purchase in 1964, he argued with an indignant used car salesman in South Philadelphia, that the sleek Ford Galaxie 500 my Dad had in mind was all show and not worth its price of $2,600. Would anyone pay $2,600 for the classy stylings of a Ford *Shit*? That was the question Grandpop Tony posed, arguing if he took his screwdriver and removed the word '*Galaxie*' and replaced it with '*Shit*' the salesman would be hard pressed to make any sale at all.

Who would pay $2,600 for a Ford Shit?

Needless to say, Grandpop Tony was asked to leave the car lot. My Dad may not have gotten a car that day, but he got a story that made for a lifetime of laughs.

Everyone loved him, all his nieces and nephews, loads of people who went on to make more people, everyone loved him, even on his grumpy days – and of those, there were many. He was confident yet unsettled. Perturbed, yet humorous. Antisocial, yet friendly. Withdrawn, and at the same time, ready to tell stories for hours – and laugh the whole time.

Grandpop Tony did not belong here – not this place, not this time. Not my Maine. And certainly not today.

So, why is he here?

It was two years ago I found out I had cancer. It was three months ago it came back after a cruel sabbatical and now, with my system managing to function with chemical imbalances in my bloodstream, I had to wonder – was I dead? Did I drop dead on the trail minutes ago? Did I see Sammie at all? Was this my grandfather? Was this even Maine?

Was I even still me?

"I'm tellin' ya, you are gonna drive yourself nuts if you keep talkin like that, worryin, worryin, worryin. What are you worryin for? What's the worst thing that can happen to you? You're either walking with me, and you're alive. Or you're walking with me, and you're dead. Either way, I'm with you, so forget about it – pay attention to right now. Don't try to guess anything. You never know, anything can happen, like snow into April," my grandfather said as he splintered the silence of our walk. "Do you remember me telling you that – it could snow into April?"

I nodded.

I remembered.

When I was a little girl, on a blustery February day in New Jersey, I looked out the living room window to see my brother and kids from the neighborhood playing in deep snow. It was the kind of snow every kid wished for as soon as the first sting of December air hits. It was the snow of tunnel digging, fort building and monstrous snowmen – the kind that would take weeks to melt.

On this winter morning, I had a fever and sore throat which meant, of course, that I was not building any snowmen. Leaning over the back of the couch that propped against the windows of my childhood home, facing out over the front lawn, all I could do was watch the fun of a snow day. It was then that my grandfather propped himself knees first onto the couch cushions and took the same stance as did I, pensively leaning over the couch with my face so close to the window I could feel the cold on my nose.

He asked me what was wrong.

Annoyed, because it was obvious to me, even at age eight, that anyone could see that I was dejected over my missed snow fun, I responded to him without even looking at his face.

"I'm sick, Mom says I can't play in the snow today – I am missing everything," my little girl voice broke the words to him. "I can't go outside. I am stuck in here. It's not fair."

He seemed unapologetically matter of fact. "What are you worried about, it snows into April, you'll have plenty of chances to go out in the snow," he told me.

"Really?" I said, turning my head to see his face was inches from mine. "It really snows into April? All the way into April, but that's like springtime. That's almost Easter time."

"Sure, it can snow in April," he said. "It can snow a lot in April; you have plenty of time."

With that, I felt better. I could feel my little body, still in cotton and fleece pajamas, begin to settle off the back of the couch. No longer pushing my childhood frame against the back of the couch, lurching over the top of it to meet the window, I could feel my shoulders drop and my arms and belly relax. I sat down in the couch, and, looking away from the window for the first time in over an hour, I felt better. My small frame relaxed. I was no longer in despair.

It could snow into April.

There was hope.

As we walked the trail, I told him of course I remembered him telling me that snow days can be more than I imagined as a girl. That it could really snow into April. That sometimes when you think you are stuck, you are not – and that I could almost feel the fabric of the couch against my cheek and chin as I recalled sitting there with him, long ago.

He smiled.

"Good, I'm glad you remember that, because it's true – and not just about snow," he said to me. "Right now, me and you, here together, this is our snow day, this is like snow in April. This is our day, your day, to walk together and it don't matter if there is sun or rain or snow or whatever in this day, it is your day. It's your birthday, Penny, and it's also your day to take your walk. It's your Walk Day."

As he said the words *Walk Day* a thick summer breeze rushed over us and caused the leaves and bushes around the narrow trail we navigated together to scatter and sway. In the breeze I heard the tingling of Sammie's collar and felt the presence of more than just my grandfather beside me. I looked beyond his shoulders and into the bushes and trees, and I thought I saw shapes, figments of lines that almost took the form of shoulders, dances of sunlight that drifted, with purpose, behind tree trunks and lingered. There were people there, almost there, and you could almost see, almost discern, their shapes in the lines of light and swaying movement of the trees.

I felt as if I was at the center of something, or on my way to the center of something, with Grandpop Tony as my guide.

"What are you looking for," Grandpop Tony said, almost laughing. "Oh, you feel them? Do you see them already? That happens sometimes."

"Penny," Grandpop Tony said thoughtfully, looking for a way to bring me up to speed. "Remember when you were a little girl, you must have been maybe six years old, just before you started first grade, and you saw a cricket for the first time in the basement? It was big and jumping around, and you were scared of it. Remember?"

"Yes," I told him. "I remember."

"So, what did I do? I got on my hands and knees and went after it. I cupped it on my hands, and I showed the cricket to you, then we pushed open the basement window and you watched me throw it out into the grass – and off that cricket went." Grandpop Tony told me. "You knew you were safe with me, and you know the cricket was not going to hurt you. You forgot about being afraid of the cricket, and you wanted me to go catch it again, and bring it back in the house, remember?"

"Yeah," I told him. "I *remember*."

He stepped closer to me. As he did, I could have sworn I heard a voice in the trees whisper *"Now,"* but it may have been my imagination or my own anticipation of what he might say next. I noticed the limp he always had, as he inched closer to me, his weakened leg, pulling behind is good one. He stood right in front of me and looked at me as if he was about to share a secret.

"Sometimes," Grandpop Tony said. "Sometimes, we can feel something is there, or we hope something is there, like when you were little with that cricket." He took my right hand in his and, for an instant, I felt like a little girl again – my hand looked smaller, my skin softer, a childlike hand almost lost in the size of his strong, tanned hands. Inexplicably, my hand was delicate, tiny and for an instant, my entire frame felt small. I felt little. And, in this moment, I felt protected.

"Your Walk Day is a very special day, Penny," he said to me. "And you have nothing to fear, from anything you see or anything you think you see. It's just like that cricket – nothing to fear."

We walked for a bit, holding hands. My hand still felt inexplicably little.

Grandpop Tony let me take it all in, the golden beams of sunlight that appeared now to swirl and dance in the trees, forming shapes like circles and even the swirls of bits of letters and designs. I thought I saw a pony. At one point, the beams danced about, and I thought I saw the shape of a bunny, then a ring, then a pair of glasses. I saw a basketball. I saw what looked like a coin. Was it a penny? Shapes and pieces of shapes were pouring out of the sunbeams that flew around Grandpop Tony and I as we continued to walk, holding hands. Fearless, and moving forward.

Grandpop Tony began to speak.

He slowed his pace a bit. The beams of sunlight slowed, as if to get in position to hear whatever he was going to say to me. "I remember my Walk Day. I was half dead, it was terrible, in my hospital bed and then my mother came to the foot of the bed, my mother, her name was Rosa, she touched my toes and, Penny, I gotta tell you, I lifted, lifted up out of that bed. I saw my sister Mary. My brother Jimmy. How do I tell you this part? I don't know how to tell you this part. I floated up, there was, how do I say this, there was a hole in the ceiling of my hospital room, right over my bed, a hole made of gold that moved like water, Penny it looked like gold waves in a tub on the ceiling above me, and my mother took me, she carried me into the gold," he told me, slowing his pace to look at my expression. "I don't know what else to tell ya," Grandpop Tony told me, shaking his head slightly from side to side, as if he was reliving his own moments of disbelief. "One minute I'm in bed, I'm almost dead, then I was no more in the hospital. I was gone, gone into the tub in the ceiling, with my mother holding my hand."

Grandpop Tony talked about South Philadelphia's historic Italian Market on 9th Street, and the entrancing rich smells of herbs, spices, fresh seafood, ground coffee, fresh fruits, and vegetables the merchants displayed, with meats, cheeses and fresh baked breads, an ocean of Italian delicacies, in overflowing quantities adorning one wooden merchant stand to the next as if rolling like waves in the sea, limitless, deep, and abundant. He talked about walking with his mother and finding his way somehow steps from the Italian Market to West Somerset Street along 21st Street where sat the home the Philadelphia Athletics, Shibe Park. Demolished in July of 1976, Shibe Park opened on April 12, 1909, as the Philadelphia Athletics took their first Shibe Park victory over the Boston Red Sox.

Then, his walk with his mother landed him looking up at a larger-than-life mural of one-time Philadelphia Major Frank Rizzo looking out over South Philadelphia. He recalled a surprisingly quick scene where he and his mother walked along Passyunk Avenue, anchoring themselves for a long while by South Philly landmark known as "Singing Fountain" on Easy Passyunk Avenue at the intersection of Tasker and 11th Streets. There, they listened to the sounds of Frank Sinatra booming from the fountain's speakers. As his time with his mother grew shorter, and the sun began to sink into the Delaware River, Grandpop Tony found himself watching the 1976 New Year's Day Mummer's Parade, watching the Ferko String Band march inches from them, boisterous and proud, in red, white, and blue in celebration of their theme, *The Spirit of 76*. After watching a few more string bands strut by, Grandpop Tony and his mother were back at St. Agnes Hospital at South Broad and Mifflin Streets, where he died.

"Are you ok?" I asked him.

I could see he was still absorbing his own experience, his memories still raw, and, despite being the host of my own unbelievable experience, I could see he still carried disbelief in his own. Grandpop Tony squeezed my hand, which remained small, impossibly childlike, in his course and strong hand.

"That was something I'll never forget, my mother and me. She was with me the whole time, Penny, but I saw my grandfather, I saw my brothers, but they looked like kids. I saw your father as a baby. I held him again, my son. I ate ripe cherries, and we drank wine. We were walking everywhere, my mother and me. My mother wanted me to know, my death would not be my end. She wanted me to know, my dying, it was a beginning. She told me *Morirai figlio mio, ma vivrai*."

"What does that mean?" I asked him.

"She told me, in Italian, *you are going to die, my son, but you are going to live*."

"Wait," I said to him. "Am I dying? Right now? Am I dead?"

"Do you feel dead?" he asked me, stopping to wait for my reply.

"I don't feel dead," I almost whispered his way, waiting for him to correct me. I wondered if that was the right answer. I also wondered if maybe all this was a dehydration-induced hallucination, because, if it was, it was magnificently detailed. I found myself making a mental note to ask my doctor if hallucinations were going to be an escalating worry.

Then I shifted my eyes toward Grandpop Tony.

His facial expression said it all. Crooked smile, eyebrows up in amusement, head tilted.

"Penny, you are not dead," he told me, as he began to stride forward. "I was not dead for my walk; you are not dead for your walk. No one is dead on their Walk Day and, guess what, dead is not really what you think it is either – not really. Being dead is no like anybody thinks, we're all knuckleheads."

"So, this is my Walk Day? On my birthday, it's my Walk Day?" I asked him.

"It's funny you have your birthday today, it's good though, it makes this Walk Day even more special for you and I guess it makes your birthday more special too, yeah? I think so," Grandpop Tony said to me.

"This experience, this *Walk Day*?" I asked him. "Is this something everyone gets, whatever this is, this Walk Day? This is a thing, a real thing?"

"Yes, and no," he said. "I don't have all the answers, but what I can tell you is that most of us, in our lives, not all people, but most, get a Walk Day. It's just how it all works. People don't talk about it, or they don't remember it – or they don't wanna remember it. Sometimes they can't remember it. I don't blame the ones who don't want to remember though, because not all walks are good ones."

Taking one step after the other, our pacing matched as if choreographed, Grandpop Tony and I continued our conversation.

Grandpop Tony talking.

I, beyond all belief, listening.

The more we walked, the better I felt, as if every step was a dose of medicine, healing me.

"I have been on many walks with people, Penny, all kinds, friends, family," Grandpop Tony explained. "For each of my sisters. My sister Mary's walk was the longest I have been on so far. Some of my brothers. My nephews, Joe, and Dominic. For your father, he don't remember his though – but that's how it goes sometimes. Sometimes we remember, sometimes we don't. I don't know if you will remember anything I'm saying to you right now. Your father's walk happened during one of his surgeries years ago – that walk was a long one, too. Some remember, some don't. Some see their walk in their dreams, some just think they are dreaming. Sometimes, people don't wanna take their walk, they run from it, avoid it, anything they can do to shut their eyes to it. Not you though, not you. That's good. That's really good."

"I wasn't sure what was going on, I still don't know what's going on," I said, feeling more like my age of 55, the tiny hand in Grandpop Tony's now seemed larger, and more worn. I felt taller, more myself, and less myself at the same time. "I'm sorry I didn't tell you I love you more. We all missed you when you left us, and I'm sorry if, before you went, you didn't know how important you were to me."

He shook his head slightly, little movement left, then right, then left again, almost in slow motion, as if he were hearing something he rejected. As he moved his head, I could have sworn I saw the lightest glimmers of what looked to be gold dust gently falling from his lower cheeks and, from his chin, speckled out in little golden pops into the air.

"Walk Days are not about regret – don't you regret nothin when it comes to me. I loved you, you, and your brother, I loved being there to see you come up, and watch you grow, and seeing you begin. I loved every minute I had to be a part of it and, when it was my time to go, I was good knowing that your grandmother would be there for a long time after me to watch you grow up even more."

My grandmother.

Would I see her today?

Grandmom Philly was a decade younger than my grandfather and so, when Grandpop Tony died at 68 she was just three years older than I was right now. Suddenly, the age of 58 felt less ancient. I never realized what a young widow she was, it never occurred to me. She lived for more than twenty years after he died so she did get to see my brother and I grow up. She did get to be a part of our lives for a long time – much longer than Grandpop Tony. Grandmom Philly saw the proms, high school plays, graduations, heartbreaks, achievements, college acceptances and then the college graduations. She was around to give her two cents on all the ups and downs that come with growing up, with growing older.

I found myself, standing with Grandpop Tony, in the new silence that we shared willingly, somehow both of us in a mutual pause as we remembered Grandmom Philly. The sounds of nature began to slowly integrate into our shared state of thought, that seemed for both of us to be an odd combination of lachrymose and joy. With the melodiousness of nature further surrounding us with its musicality, we found each of us began to look around a bit, perceptive of the aria that played for us from them bedrock of the desolate Maine trail.

I wondered if he was looking for Grandmom Philly in the thick of the trees. We began our slow pace over the terrain with our feet walking on the dirt as if we were gliding over a marble pedestal, somehow drifting forward over solid ground, yet unable to corrupt it.

Were we on unworldly land? Is he really here with me in this sainted, solitary space? Are we walking or floating like a sprite or seraph? I think maybe we are celestial beings.

"You think a lot, you think too much," his words broke my illation.

"You know how it snows in April sometimes," he asked me as the trail took a slight bend to the right. "You know what the really is about, what the thought of snowing in April really means?"

I shook my head, partly because I wasn't sure what he was getting at, and mostly because I was still in awe of speaking to him.

"It means never give up hope," he told me, stopping to take both of my hands in his tanned, tough fingers. "It means to always know it could snow into April, and always be open to keeping that knowledge and hope in your heart. It means that anything is possible – and to never let one day, or one bad experience, or one disease, make you feel like there is no time ahead to do all the things you dream of doing."

I looked into his eyes and felt the tears welling in my own, because I somehow could feel my time with him was stepping to an end.

"It snows into April," I said to him.

"It snows into April," he said back to me, closing his eyes and smiling.

Just then, two voices interrupted us. It was the booming voice of one man, and the softer voice of a second. I could hear their voices getting closer as the trees and grass gave away their direction.

"Toooooony! Toooooony!" the booming voice called out. "It's time to go, we're playin cards. Hurry up." The men seemed to stop a short distance away, staying within the thickness of the tree line off the tiny trail on which my grandfather and I stood. I could see their silhouettes glittering in the beams of sunlight that hit their shoulders. One man was very big. He was the loudest. "Tony, let's go, Mikey is here, and Joe is waiting for us to get started."

I knew the voices, despite the barrage of undetectable words they were uttering to one another, out there in the sunbeams. They could not hide the familiarity of their inflections, the tone of their pitches, or the hints of their personalities.

I knew the voices very well.

The voices were memories – echoes from decades gone.

It was my Uncle Jimmy, my Grandpop Tony's older brother, and the Mikey could only be their youngest brother, Uncle Mike. The *Joe* my Uncle Jimmy, actually both he and Uncle Mikey were my great uncles, referred to could only be one of their most favorite nephews, their sister Jenny's son – and playing cards was something all were known for in the family.

That, and being devoted to each other.

Jimmy was a massive man; I knew him well in my childhood. A protector of the family, once known for being one of the fiercest street fighters in South Philly – a husband, a devoted father, a relentless and loving grandfather. He took family seriously, rooted in the ties to Calabria that were the framework of his and my grandfather's Italian upbringing. Uncle Jimmy was a gentle giant of a guy. Uncle Mikey was more gentle than giant, the most handsome of all the brothers, none of which were bad looking, but none with the beautiful features that Uncle Mike possessed. He was slow to participate in conversation, but was always listening.

Uncle Mike, to one who did not know him, could seem adrift, in his own world, even oblivious, but his service in World War II was a reminder to all that, under his soft voice and kind, distracted demeanor, there was a heart of valor and a soul that had seen atrocities unimaginable to most. Uncle Mike was present, but somehow lost. With you, and a million miles away. A soldier, a husband, a father, and a victim.

These were the voices in the woods right now.

Uncle Jimmy.

Uncle Mikey.

These were the men calling out to my grandfather. They were making their presence known to me, calling out for him, but straining and stretching to get a glimpse of me – and I them. I could see my Uncle Jimmy nodding his head methodically up and down as if approving of seeing me, and Uncle Mikey, with his angelic face painted with a faraway, lost expression that he brought home from the war, staring at me through the wind-tossed leaves, smiling at me, a tear of gold I thought I saw gently sparkle down his right cheek – it was an unbelievable reunion, utterly natural, or supernatural, and implausibly divine.

Would I see my Grandpop Tony's sisters too?

"I'll see you again at the end of your Walk Day," Grandpop Tony told me. "You keep going down the trail and you'll see who is waiting for you next. Don't be afraid, and don't stop walking forward – no matter what you see," he told me, beginning to position his shoulders away and move toward the voices of his brothers. "I'm coming Jimmy, hold on," he yelled out, with an eyeroll.

With that, he stepped slowly away, looking at me until he needed to turn his head forward to navigate the thickness of the trees, stumps, and bushes. I heard his feet crunching the dried brush and tiny sticks that carpeted his pathway, until he reached his brothers and their silhouettes drifted into sparkling particles that melted into pillars of sunbeams that cut into the wooded trail.

"Happy Birthday Penny," Grandpop Tony's voice carried over the breeze. I saw Uncle Mikey, who died when I was 12, reach his hand up as if to wave me forward, pushing at the air in my direction as he drifted into sunbeams with his brothers, the contours of their heads, shoulders and even Uncle Mikey's fingertips as he waved me forward, spinning and churning together into streams of gold.

Until they were gone.

"It snows into April," I said out loud, and, with that, I started to walk slowly, deeper down the trail ahead. Before I took my first step forward, not knowing what or who was waiting for me down the tiny trail, I spotted something shinning from the gravel below me. It was a penny. A sparkling, untouched before right now penny. I bent down, picked up the penny and turned it over and over, admiring its newness, its freshly minted pristine appearance.

Only thing, there was no date on the penny – how could that be? Was this penny just for me? Does time not matter for this penny? Or me? Holding my new penny, I looked up at the treetops.

"Thank you, Grandpop," I said to the air.

I said to *him*. I placed my new penny in my jeans pocket, and, with a quick lift of my backpack, took my next steps. I felt uplifted and ready to move forward.

A lucky penny, indeed.

The Steps

Your mind wanders when you are walking.

I was born at Pennsylvania Hospital on a crisp August morning, the first of two, to parents who were little more than kids themselves. My Dad was just 18 when he met my mother, only 15, on a beach in Atlantic City and when the boy with a roaring personality from South Philly met the shy girl from Upland, Pennsylvania, and it was love at first sight.

For some, love at *first* sight happens – two souls connect, or reconnect if you believe in the pull of past life energy or divine intervention, each soul seeking the other with an inexplicable longing that manifests without warning. For my parents, it was love at first sight. They married three years later, my mother just 18 and my father all of 21 and little more than two years from their wedding day they were parents.

Homeowners. Taxpayers. Grown Ups.

Two kids, clinging on to each other to grow up together as they started all the chores and tasks of adulthood, in a different time, when adulthood hit earlier than it does today for most. How fortunate was I that, earlier this year, I was able to celebrate with them their 57 years of married life, and that, despite the health obstacles they endured in their most recent, and sadly final year together, they were still, on the day their union turned 57, two kids in love, clinging to one another, still growing up in this world together.

The South Philly boy with the roaring personality. The shy girl from Upland. A lifetime of building a lifetime, all in the tiny moments of 57 years as one.

I wondered what they would think if they knew I talked to Grandpop Tony today. Lost in thought, drifting over the conversation I just had with my long-deceased grandfather, I realized I had no clue how long I had been walking the trail alone. I found myself wondering.

Did I imagine everything?

My dog.

Grandpop Tony.

The uncles in the woods.

The surreal sunbeams.

The trail was quiet and remained a smaller carved out pathway of a trail that looked as though it was well traveled decades ago and, with the expansion of larger trails throughout Acadia National Park, somehow lost its usefulness.

You could see the path get almost inches wide at times, as it carved its way into the dirt – refusing to disappear.

As I moved through the wooded sanctuary of a forest I looked up at the towering spruce and pine trees filling my horizon. After walking these spruce, pine and cedar covered trails for more than two decades with my own young family, I thought I had explored all the more popular, and even some lesser known, trails Acadia had to offer.

I was wrong.

With each step, I felt pulled forward, deeper into an unfamiliar weaving of forest tapestry, almost removed from the Acadia landscape so familiar to me.

It would be very easy to get lost on this trail.

As I moved just steps beyond a remarkably tall spruce, I stopped in awe. Within a few feet of me, on this dirt trail, tucked into gold-soaked woods, there stood an impossible sight. As I gazed on the unbelievable, Sammie's sound, her very essence, was somehow back, faint but there – ting, ting, ting. Ting, ting, ting. It was back, the tingling, the ting, ting, tingling of her collar bells accompanied by the delicate patter of her puttering, pattering excited paws near me.

How it was, on this deep and winding wooded trail, I found myself standing in front of the South Philadelphia row house my grandmother grew up in was beyond my understanding, at this point, but with all I had seen, it was not beyond my acceptance. There before me, there I saw the impossible.

The red bricks of an aged city house I had not seen in decades. The compact, immaculately beaming marble and concrete South Philly stoop that somehow broke out of the trees and bushes of the overgrown Maine trail, as if it, and the red brick house it guarded, had been built there, grew old there – *lived there.*

In South Philadelphia, one chore that was paramount to keeping your house in order was making sure your front step was pristine. It was a laborious job. It was repetitive. It was tiring. It was dirty.

It was important.

The South Philly rowhouse that stood before me boasted a top step that was almost illuminated, as if every step that composed the radiance that was the very structure of the stoop was electrified – beaming with a flawlessness that could only be achieved with a laundered mastery. Each step was unblemished, cleansed to a speckless degree so that the stoop sparkled with an unpolluted, elegant countenance reserved for works of art – or the wings of Heaven's most favored angels.

Within seconds, I heard her speak. The custodian, or perhaps guardian, of the steps.

"It only takes a minute to do something right," she said with resolve. I could hear the clinking of metal, a squeaking, clinking sound, accompanied by swishing of water until I saw her. She swayed around the side of the house, a woman of about 30 or so years, wearing a flowered pattern cotton dress, her hair pulled back and a white cotton apron tied just below her waist, sitting more on her very full hips. The apron, which I could see was tightly tied, had roses on its only pocket, which sat over her left thigh. She walked toward me carrying the swishing, clinking source of sound, a deep metal pail that overflowed with soapy water.

I had never seen her this young.

It was without a doubt my Aunt Elvira.

"Aunt … *Elvira*?" I asked, knowing what the answer would be. I walked toward her, and the house. The house was just as I remembered it. Aunt Elvira was *not*. The last time I saw her was the day after Christmas when I was 28. I stopped to visit her and drop off some groceries to her. She was 76 at the time. The next day she died unexpectedly.

Yet here she was, right now, younger than I am in this moment – and very busy.

She put the pail down, reached into it and pulled out a soaked cloth. "I gave them a good scrubbing before you got here, just finishing up," she told me, as she wiped down the steps. I could see she must have swept the steps first, as a beaten wood-handled and thickly woven horsehair broom leaned against the bricks of the house.

"It only takes a minute to do something right," she said to me, as she placed her right hand on the impeccably white top step. I remembered her saying the same thing to me throughout my childhood. When changing sheets on a bed. When folding bath towels fresh from the dryer. When mopping the kitchen floor before a holiday or big family event. When painting my fingernails or ironing a dress. Whatever the task, Aunt Elvira promoted poise, equanimity, and diligence. She was all about the art of grit under pressure, keeping a hint of hauteur in everything you do, being prideful, but not self-important in your air. If you were doing a task wrong, she corrected you.

Typically, if you weren't doing it her way, you were doing it wrong.

"I always told you, you can manage anything, any chore, no matter how big or small, you just must take your time. It only takes one minute to do something right," she said, her blue eyes almost electric, seemingly sparkling in the fine sunlight beam that illuminated her enthused expression.

Aunt Elvira was a woman ahead of her time. Outspoken. Fiercely independent. She may have been born in 1917, but she was rapid of mind when it came to owning her authenticity and doing whatever she had to do to secure her own, independent happiness. She would love who she loved. She would earn her own money. She would defend her family. She would hold her head high in any circumstance.

She would be impeccable – for *herself*, not anyone else.

And her steps, her South Philly stoop, would be the most impeccable on Mifflin Street.

I looked at her. I could not help myself from smiling, it was so good to see her, and I missed seeing her.

Aunt Elvira was actually my great-great aunt.

She and my Grandmom Philly, also her niece, were only a few years apart – more like sisters, with Elvira being a surprise addition to an already overcrowded hatchery of Italian siblings, the oldest of which was my great-grandmother, Esther, mother to my Grandmom Philly. Aunt Elvira was generations removed from me, but, at the same time, somehow, a fitting and relevant contemporary, a woman with high adoration of her value in the world, not as someone's wife, or daughter, or sister, or even aunt, but as the uniquely formed creation that was uniquely her.

At a time when most women aspired to be locally celebrated homemakers, managing majestic little houses with the latest vacuum cleaners and Tupperware, shuffling a gaggle of neatly dressed and perfectly behaved children to church on Sundays, only to dazzle her hardworking husband and collection of majestic kids with a four-course Sunday dinner, Aunt Elvira was a radiant contradiction. She enjoyed nightclubs. She danced into the early mornings. She supported herself and contributed to the family household by working in a textile factory. She purchased lipsticks and perfumes, not baby booties and bow ties.

Most important, she was *content*. She determined her own pleasure, spent time with the people closest to her heart, and enjoyed the drama, vibrancy and even scandalously surging excitement of a woman managing herself in the world. On her own terms. In her own time. Fully satisfied. Aunt Elvira handled her life on her terms, until her seven decades of mindful independence came to an end. Until that time, she handled her money, her body, her life. She handled it all, her way.

"You can handle your life too, you can handle anything, as long as you take a minute," Aunt Elvira broke my thoughts. "How you handle that minute, Penny, that is up to you - it is always up to you. I always told you, your strength does not come from what happens to you, it comes from how you face what happens to you, how you create what happens to you – how you do right, by you."

Aunt Elvira was always one to call it like she saw it.

"We've all been watching you, you know, and we're all proud of you except, lately you haven't really been doing right by you, have you, Penny?" Aunt Elvira asked. "Not really, right? You're down. You need to work on that and stand up straight. You are slouching bad Penny; you look all hunched – not good. That's gonna make you look old, you don't want that, Penny, you're not a kid anymore, you're up there now. Looking old is not what you want to do, trust me."

With that heartfelt directive, she picked up the dented, metal pail filled with now filthy, thick water and dumped it in the bushes next to the brilliantly white stoop. Placing the empty metal pail on the dirt, she wiped her wet hands against her cotton apron and began walking into the house, but not before she, for my benefit, she overexaggerated pulling her shoulders back, pushing her breasts forward and holding her chin up so that her brilliant blue eyes caught a sunbeam as she posed for my benefit. She winked at me, but kept her chin facing upwards, bobbing her head from side to side as if to pull my attention even more to her squared shoulders.

"Come on, you don't have much time, and you have more of your Walk Day to do. You saw your grandfather, yes? That was what we all agreed, Tony would start your day," she said as she opened the door. "I have something for you – come with me Penny, try not to track too much dirt. Are those your best shoes for walking? Really? They are kind of ugly. They don't have any style. They make you look old. And what's going on with your hair? What happened to your hair, it used to be so pretty Penny, you used to keep it so nice. What's going on, up there."

She gestured to her own meticulously sleek hair, pointing her finger at her own head, moving it about a bit, as if to demonstrate how human hair should display, then swirling her finger around the air to my head, and separating her fingers in a spread-out motion, as if trying to recoil.

"You have to keep yourself nice, Penny," Aunt Elvira told me, with an abruptness that almost made me forget the joy of seeing her again. "You have to put yourself first. You have to take the time to look your best, people will judge you. They don't care if you're sick, nobody cares if you can't sleep or if you are too tired to take a shower. People will look at you, so you look your best. This ain't it. This ain't it, not at all. You used to be so pretty, Penny, what happened?"

Did I say I missed Aunt Elvira?

With that, she bounded up the gloriously white steps, placed her hand on the knob of the green wooden door, and opened it, giving it an added push so that it hit the wall behind it, exposing the foyer and, ahead, what was the entry door into the living room – just as I remembered it from my childhood. When you walked into a house in South Philly, you typically walked into a foyer, more appropriately termed by all Philadelphians as a vestibule.

In South Philadelphia, vestibules mattered greatly. Going back as far as the first rowhouses built in the city, stretching back before Benjamin Franklin uttered most of his famous quotes, pushing back time to 1690 or so, Philadelphia's rowhouses were born.

Originally inspired by northern European and British cities, the early days of Philadelphia growing from expansive land of promise to bustling city started with rows and rows of individual houses sharing common side walls and roof. Within these houses, of all sizes, vestibules were fixtures of necessity, convenience, and stature. They were a person's first exposure to a house, once through the front door. Some vestibules were small. Some large and grandly attired. In modern times, some homeowners in Philadelphia opt to remove vestibules from their homes to gain floor space.

What a pity.

The vestibule of the South Philly home I was somehow standing in on this uneven, scraggy patch of remote Maine trail, was only a few feet in narrow length, just enough to do its most important job as a vestibule of catching rain, stopping blasts of cold air and repelling snowy gusts from pushing into the house. The vestibule was where you wiped your feet, shook off your coat on inclement days, and tossed down your umbrella. It was where you readied yourself to go into the house. The vestibule I now stood in was unboastful by design, but functional in every respect.

People don't appreciate vestibules anymore.

"Alright," Aunt Elvira said, looking over her right shoulder at me. "Let's go."

As she opened the vestibule's door, she moved forward from it and into the main body of the first floor of the rowhouse that once was – *or remains* – her home. She seemed to glide out of the tiny vestibule and sway into house, which responded to her by lighting up as she moved forward, deeper into it. This Mifflin Street rowhouse was a modest two stories, first floor with vestibule, living room, dining room, kitchen and a small summer kitchen mounted to the back of the structure to keep the heat of cooking out of the main house – especially in summer. The upstairs supported one small bathroom and three bedrooms. At its height of service to my bloodline, this Mifflin Street house was home to more than 14 family members at one time. As the decades went forward, eventually, Aunt Elvira was the last family member to occupy the house.

Being alone was not a problem for Aunt Elvira.

I started up the immaculately white steps behind her, to walk through a doorway that I had not seen in decades. A doorway that should not be here, on the dirt, in Maine. A doorway to a Mifflin Street house in South Philadelphia where my Grandmom Philly was raised, where Aunt Elvira was raised and where my father played as a boy. The house that saw my Grandmom Philly stand in its front doorway for her wedding pictures. The same structure that laid to rest relatives I had never even met. The first home to welcome the birth of my father. The house where my family surprised me with a Sweet Sixteen birthday celebration.

The house in which I learned my Grandpop Tony had died.

Am I dead now?

Steps behind a buoyant Aunt Elvira, I walked through the tiny vestibule and looked into the house. As Aunt Elvira walked further from the vestibule and deeper into the house, the home's windows came alive with sunlight pouring through every hint and corner of glass, separating the now glowing house from the stoic Maine trail on which it miraculously and inexplicably sat.

The walls glowed with a golden hue that appeared like thinly poured honey from ceiling to carpet. The windows illuminated as if the sun itself was outside of each one, yet somehow the light was bearable, even nourishing. The air was filled with little bits of gold that seemed to pop and crackle out of nowhere before disappearing.

As my eyes scanned this familiar, and eerily unfamiliar space, I caught whispers of sunlight, hushed hues of yellow and gold, decorating the house or, perhaps, awakening it. I also felt a buzz in the air, a hushed tone that was not quite a mumble or mutter, but more like a low frequency vibration – tingling up my body from my feet and ankles to my shoulders, neck, and temples, as if carrying a secret message only my body could understand.

As I stepped deeper into the house, there they all were – frozen, like a picture. I saw my Grandmom Philly first, standing motionless by the dining room table.

She was holding a plate of what looked to be fried chicken cutlets, readying to put it on the table, which was already overwhelmed with serving plates abundant with food. She was motionless, or rather, as I watched her for a few seconds, it was clear she was moving very, very slowly. Almost imperceptible, Grandmom Philly's movements were so finely intangible they were apparitional, as her shoulders seemed to dip closer to the table, and the corners of her mouth ever so slightly seemed to move upwards. She appeared to be pushing through space and time to meet the illuminated pace of Aunt Elvira.

Aunt Elvira fluttered closer to Grandmom Philly and the others, all seemingly motionless, to take her seat, joining them at the table for what looked to be a family dinner. As Aunt Elvira continued her motion, the beams of sunlight garnishing the room bloomed with color. I saw hairs move across faces, like a gentle wind was rushing over them – not me. The blossoming sunbeams overtook the table and its occupants, with light bouncing off the glasses and plates set out. Within a few more seconds, or maybe minutes, I'm not sure, I could see that the ample serving plate my Grandmom Philly held with both of her hands was now touching the top of the dining room table. I noticed my Aunt Elvira smiling ear to ear, watching the table intently.

As sunlight painted over the entirety of the dining room, the picture came alive.

And so did Grandmom Philly.

Grandmom Philly

Whiffs of very real, enticingly hearty foods adorning the table suddenly overwhelmed me. There was the sweet aroma of fried Italian sausages, mixing with the tang of fresh parmesan cheese, the robustness of fried green peppers, and an abundant bouquet of homemade tomato sauce, or as we always called it, gravy, casting rich plumes of deliciousness old-fashioned goodness into the air.

The house was suddenly very much alive. The people were joyful. And they were all my people – every one of them, but not as I knew them. They were all younger. As Aunt Elvira joined them all at the dining room table, an antique I remembered from my youth, they all stopped talking – smiled in my direction, and welcomed me with loving expressions, as if they just noticed me.

Grandmom Philly.

Aunt Marie, her only sister. Uncle Mikey, married to Aunt Marie, and the little brother of Grandpop Tony. Grandmom Philly's mother, my great grandmother, Esther. Her father, my great grandfather, Giuseppe.

Grandmom Philly appeared to be just about my current age, give or take. She looked young, and so very real.

Before I could take a step deeper into the house toward the table, a little boy, not more than eight or nine at most, ran down the home's steep staircase from the upstairs, announcing his arrival with booming and plunking footsteps that flattened the serenity framing this impossible room. Before hitting the last three steps he jumped into the air, hurling himself forward and onto the floor, tumbling to his knees like an action hero, with his shirt hanging out of his jeans and his shoes untied.

"*Miiiiiiiiiiiiiichael!*" my grandmother yelled out, her piercing voice like a time machine for me, bringing me back to the countless times she would yell out to me to find my shoes, fetch her something or do some other tasks that needed to be done in a hurry. Or the countless times she would call out to me to come to dinner or see something interesting on TV.

With Grandmom Philly's voice echoing through the house, the little boy, utterly unfazed by the shouting of his name, pushed himself up, laughing as he ran over, tripping on his way, to join his parents, Aunt Marie and Uncle Mikey, and his other family at the table. I knew this little boy very well. Oh, not as a boy, of course, he was well into his teen years by the time I made my entrance. The cute little boy with the black hair and the mischievous smile. This hyper kid, with his shirt now somehow unbuttoned and half off him, his undershirt rumpled and his feet moving too fast for his body to keep up. This sweet little guy, surrounded by everyone who loved him the most.

As I watched the little boy – *Michael* – give my grandmother a hug, I took my first steps closer to this haunting collection of loving family. Moving nearer to them, my grandmother began walking toward me and when we met, she hugged me, took my hands in hers and said…

"*Penny … there you are.*"

Indeed, there I was, however impossible.

Grandmom Philly squeezed my hands tight. As she held my hands, I looked into her face, then down at my hands, which I no longer recognized. They were my hands, but from decades earlier, before the lift of life, the push of parenthood and the inevitable touch of age. I realized then that my hair was longer, thicker, and darker, with waves and whisps that gently fluttered about my temples, brushed over my eyebrows and even a whisp or two over my eyes. My back felt strong. The clothes on me were very loose. I felt smaller, yet stronger, at the same time.

The slight breeze, from somewhere that I had noticed earlier, now seemed to pass over me and Grandmom Philly, as we stood together. Me in disbelief. She in what appeared to be gratitude. My body felt resurged – free of the burden of the high-maintenance friend that was tagging along for this mystical experience.

I was a me that was no longer me.

I was a me that Grandmom Philly knew very well.

"Now," she told me. "We have to get crackin' you don't have much time with any of us and we want to make this day special for you. You're a little later than I thought you would be. We don't have much time with you now, but we'll make the most of it."

Seeing her, hearing her, as if she had never gone away, it was beyond surreal.

"We all want you to know we are with you, when you think we are not with you, when you feel like you are stuck, struggling or fighting alone, Penny, you are not," Grandmom Philly said. "Remember what I always told you, *what's easy losing is not worth having*. You are worth having, your life is worth having, Penny. You need to take care of yourself. You need to remember you are worth everything, and you need to tell yourself, even when you feel alone, that everything you go through is worth it, it's always worth it."

What was always worth it?

Me?

Life?

The strength to keep going?

The struggle?

"Exactly, yes, that's it," Grandmom Philly said, looking into my eyes.

With that, she took my soft, youthful hand, and walked me to an open seat that the table, where I sat down, next to the great grandmother I never met, and across from the little boy who I only ever knew as an adult, for what would be the strangest and yet most important meal of my life.

"Sit up straight, Penny," Aunt Elvira said, as I got comfortable in the plushness of the dining room chair. "You want to always carry yourself high, sit up straight, shoulders back. The way you put yourself out there, that's what people see. Shoulders back, head up, boobs out."

"Yes, Aunt Elvira," I replied.

I rose up in my chair, pushed my shoulders back and I could feel the act of doing so brought my chin up a bit. It was one movement, but, at the same time, a statement. I was present. I was there, with them all. Head up. Ready to experience whatever came next. Claiming my seat at the table.

"There, don't you feel better," Aunt Elvira said, gesturing to her own perfectly poised shoulders.

I did feel better.

Aunt Elvira was right.

As always.

Celery Things

I wasn't expecting to eat a big meal today.

"Alrighty, Penny, here's a plate," my Grandmom Philly said as I got comfortable in my chair, next to the hyper boy and his parents, my Uncle Mikey and Aunt Marie. Uncle Mikey was my Grandpop Tony's youngest brother, and one of the voices I heard calling out to my grandfather off the trail. His wife, my Aunt Marie, was my Grandmom Philly's sister – two brothers marrying two sisters, a family deeply woven and, evidently, timeless.

"You have time to eat while we talk with you and then I'll take you to where you need to go next," Grandmom Philly told me, as she simultaneously put more spaghetti on little Michael's plate.

One thing about Italian Americans in South Philadelphia is you will never be hungry around them. The table was filled with food. Ornate serving dishes filled with spaghetti and meatballs Italian sausages, there was even lasagna, roast beef, sauteed broccoli rabe with fresh garlic, a large salad ripe with red tomatoes, the chicken cutlets I watched Grandmom Philly place on the table in slow motion, and a soup I had loved as a child.

We called this amazing soup celery things soup, and it was delicious.

Peasant food at its finest, all the way from Calabria, designed by generations before the ones seated here with me now. Flour, eggs, baking powder, pepper, finely chopped celery leaves and a ridiculous amount of parmesan cheese. Nothing measured or weighed, all ingredients mixed by eye in a bowl, then like pancakes or fritters, dollop by dollop, fried in virgin olive oil, until the batter of eggs, flour and celery leaves puff up golden brown. Next, the celery things are cooled and cut into little cubes while still freshly hot, tossed in a bowl with a springle more of grated parmesan cheese and gently spooned into soup bowls, where hot chicken broth is poured over them and next thing you know ... *soup heaven.*

"Celery things," I said, almost teary-eyed as my Grandmom Philly poured steaming hot chicken broth over a bowl filled with the most delectable little pieces of bread, dotted with fresh celery, in the world. The conversations around the table were in motion, as if my presence was not only expected, but eternal – a familiar and unique piece fit straightaway to its spot, with hot soup to welcome it. I looked around the table as I picked up my spoon, readying to eat the soup of my childhood dreams. Everyone was eating. They were talking about nothing of consequence, yet the table was animated with their stories, laughter, and the chatter of the day.

Little Michael, his parents, my Grandmom Philly, her mother, and her father, were enjoying the celery things soup that was now in every bowl, except one. Aunt Elvira was still deciding if she was in the mood for celery things. This amused me, as I recalled how Aunt Elvira would make very deliberate decisions.

I looked around the table.

Grandmom Philly winked at me and, with a quick nod of her head and lift of her eyebrows, encouraged me to start eating. Then, she started talking about a neighbor, Joe Smiles (*not his real last name, but in South Philadelphia any name could be yours*) who told her that their numbers taker, Tony Dimes (*Tonys were plentiful in South Philadelphia, along with Mikes, Joes and Michaels, also Dimes was not his last name*) was in the hospital and would not be back taking daily lotto numbers for at least a week. Aunt Marie chimed in that she didn't trust him anyway, and she never wins when she plays her numbers with him. Uncle Mikey asked Aunt Elvira to pass more meatballs his way. Little Michael now had more tomato sauce on his shirt than his place. My great grandmother Esther seemed humored by the conversation, as she twirled her spaghetti around her fork, she complimented her daughters on how good everything tasted. She told her husband not to eat too much because his stomach was bothering him all day.

Aunt Elvira commented that she thought the celery things looked a little dry.

Aunt Marie told her to shut her mouth.

I allowed myself to lean into the lull of the table conversation, and as I put another heaping spoonful of celery things soup to my lips, I found myself feeling completely at home.

I now fully realized that people did not have to be *dead* to be a part of this experience, as my cousin Michael, the little boy seated right across the table from me, was alive and well, and, at 15 years ahead of me in life, already retired and enjoying time with his favorite things: Hunting, cooking and discussing anything that had to do with his only son, who recently joined the military. Yet, here was Michael, a little boy, but the Michael I grew up looking up to, nonetheless.

I imagined my Grandpop Tony would typically be here, especially with all around the table being the ages they *seemed* to be. My Grandpop Tony, and my father, likely as a teenager, would fit perfectly in this particular moment. I wondered if my presence here displaced them, or if they were in some other part of this unfolding Walk Day experience.

Was there not enough room at the table now?

"How's your soup," my Aunt Elvira asked, as she sprinkled more parmesan over her steaming hot bowl. Clearly, she decided she was in the mood for celery things. "Wonderful … yes? It's so good, isn't it? Put more cheese on yours, it's even better with more cheese."

The soup, unsurprisingly, was glorious. The celery things were soft and filled with flavor. The richness of the parmesan cheese. The freshness of the finely chopped celery leaves. The heat of the black pepper. The rich flavor of the olive oil. With every spoonful I remembered the calming influence of this simple soup, made with the most basic of ingredients, costing pennies to produce – yet exquisite and, what's more, soul nourishing.

With each spoonful, I felt more settled, more comfortable, and more a part of the setting in which I found myself. Seated, at a familiar table, with family who should not be here – in this place, with me. When I finished my soup, my Aunt Elvira cleared my soup bowl and before I could say a word, my Grandmom Philly and Aunt Elvira began filling my plate with spaghetti and meatballs, with Aunt Elvira spooning grated parmesan over the entire plate.

Is this why I was here?

To have my last meal?

Is this my last supper?

If so, thanks for the celery things, God.

"This is not your last supper," Grandmom Philly said to me. "Don't think that way."

"Grandmom," I said to her, putting my fork down with spaghetti already rolled around its prongs. "You know I love you. You also know, I think you know anyway, that I'm, well, I'm struggling. I'm fighting, but I'm struggling. I'm 55 now Grandmom, right now – today, in fact, I'm not the same anymore. I am pushing forward, but I'm so, so tired and really, Grandmom, I can only do what I can do. I can only do what the doctors tell me, and it's up to God, really. I don't want you to worry or get upset with me, with whatever this is all about today, but I might be ready to just, to just be over all this, all this mess and sickness and worry and stress. I'm tired…maybe I'm *ready*?"

The table fell silent.

Even Little Michael.

No laughter. No conversation. No pouring of wine. No clinking of utensils to plates. No one was eating celery things soup. Looking into my grandmother's eyes, I finished my statement. The thick silence in the room pushed me to feeling that I needed to clarify my words. Explain why I just *might* be ready … to stop fighting to live. Explain why I just might be ready to sit at this table, with my celery things soup, and listen to them all talk about nothing, and everything, forever.

It was then that I heard my Grandpop Tony come into the house.

"*Girl?*" he called out for my Grandmom Philly.

He always called her Girl.

"Girl are you almost ready. Penny needs to keep going." I heard his voice, but did not see him, as he called out from the vestibule and, once he gave his message, I heard the squeak of the thick wooden front door as he pulled it closed.

With all still silent, I continued.

"I am not a quitter. I want to be there for my kids, and to be there to just experience whatever I am meant to experience, but Grandmom, you know I can only do what I can do – the rest is in God's hands, or my doctor's hands, or whatever the universe has in store for me, just like you had your time, your journey," I said, looking around the table at the faces looking back at me.

Just then, everyone got up from their seats and came over to give me a hug.

Uncle Mikey.

Aunt Marie.

Little Michael.

Aunt Elvira.

My grandmother's parents.

All hugged me.

All smiled and touched my hands, my hair, my forehead as each walked from the dining room, into the kitchen, that was now awash in glowing gold light. As each stepped into the kitchen, they seemed to glisten and sparkle into silhouettes of gold. The last gesture I saw of little Michel was what looked like a handstand, his feet kicking in the air as his whole little body drifted into glistening specks of sunshine. The light from the kitchen further illuminated the dining room and poured over the antique dining room table that had only two remaining occupants.

Grandmom Philly.

And me.

"I think it's time for our walk now, Penny." my grandmother said to me.

With that, we got up from the table, and walked toward the front door of the house.

We held hands as we walked through the room, with each step we took, the sunbeams, vibrantly enlivening the room, gradually dimmed, then extinguished. I noticed that, by the time we crossed the threshold and stepped onto the immaculately white steps on our way to the dirt path, my hands were older, my hair shorter and Grandmom Philly was somehow older too. Much older.

No longer a woman in her fifties, she looked as I remembered her last. A woman well into her seventies. More delicate. More determined. Her hair still mostly black, but thinner and decorated by gray strands around her temples. Her face beautifully wrinkled and aged, with her eyes on mine, she reached out her thin hand and I reached quickly for it, noticing the age that was once again decorating my own hand.

"Let me lean on you as we walk together," she told me.

"I might do more of the learning," I laughed, half serious, mostly astonished.

Grandmom Philly and I stepped slowly, leaning on one another, onto the gravel and twig-filled dirt trail that seemed to clear before us. As we took a few steps, I adjusted my backpack over my shoulder, and, in doing so, turned to see the South Philly house of her childhood, the house that my Aunt Elvira proudly cleaned, the house I visited many times in my youth, the house that still smelled like celery things, was no longer there, all remnants of it returned to its place in time.

The ring of Aunt Elvira's dented metal pail still etched in the dirt where she had placed her emptied pail earlier. No sign of her broom. No hint of the steps. No green door to ascend toward.

"The house, Grandmom, the house is gone," I told my Grandmom Philly.

"No, Penny, it's not," she said to me. "Now, get yourself together, we're late."

Running Away

When I was about five, I got very mad at my grandmother. I don't remember why. It may have had to do with a lack of peanut butter for my PB&J or her insistence that I take a nap. Whatever it was, I was having none of it.

Unfortunately, neither was Grandmom Philly.

It was a stalemate. Refusing to forfeit, and determined to have my win, I announced I was leaving – moving out, running away from home. With my mother and father at work, and my brother just a baby, I could easily make my exit, especially if I timed it during my grandmother's afternoon 'stories' which started with Young and the Restless and entertained her straight to Guiding Light.

I packed my bag.

I think, socks, some underwear and potato chips. Clearly, I was heading out for a massive adventure. Until I carried my red Muppets tote to the front door, at which point I was thwarted. "I'm running away," I told Grandmom Philly, emphatically.

"Oh," she said. "You are, Penny, well fine – go on. See ya, I'll let your parents know."

What?!! Her response outraged me. There I was, establishing my independence. Ready to fight for my liberty to express myself or, at the very least, get more peanut butter. Grandmom Philly then began to ignore me, which only made me angrier with her. How dare she? Didn't she see me standing there? Indignant. Clutching my travel tote. Ready to bolt. Ready to get out of there.

"Fine," I told her.

"Fine," she told me right back. "I don't know where you think you are going."

Truth was, I had no idea where I was going – only that I wanted to go somewhere. I wasn't sure what I wanted, or what I expected her to do or say to me. In the end, I unpacked my socks, underwear, and potato chips, slightly crushed – the chips, and me. I had no idea why I was so mad, so frustrated and, mostly, so sleepy. Looking back, I was a kid who needed a nap, with or without extra peanut butter. I needed to settle myself, appreciate her love – and unpack.

I was doing a lot of unpacking today.

As we walked through the beautiful trail together, arm in arm, walking in step and leaning on one another like a two-person army against the world, I flashed back to my insistence to run away. Without thinking through the consequences of my actions – just acting on my gut response to whatever was happening in that moment.

My actions were raw, unapologetically childish. They were also overwhelmingly selfish. As I leaned against her a touch more I asked, "Do you think I am being selfish? Do you think, that because I am accepting that I am sick, that I may not recover – do you think I am giving up, running away?"

Grandmom Philly looked sharply at me.

"C'mon Penny, now, that's not what this is about."

She didn't speak those words to me.

I just heard them.

The next part, she spoke loud and clear, giving me what was on her mind with no leniency.

"No, that's not what I think and that's not what I want you to think. What's easy losing is not worth having, you know that and there is nothing easy about losing your life," Grandmom Philly told me, gripping my arm tighter. "I don't think you are running away or giving up. I think you are scared, and you are hiding that from everyone in your life – which makes you very, very brave. You are not selfish, but you are tired – I can see how tired you are and, because you are tired, you may not be working as hard as you can to keep yourself positive. You are not telling yourself that what's easy losing is not worth having – and your life is worth having."

What's easy losing is not worth having.

Where did Grandmom Philly hear that, I should have asked her? As we continued walking the path together, me hanging on her every word, reminded me of the importance of treating yourself like your body was a temple, in that our bodies are not only our own, but also of God. The strength and power of faith, whether an eternal belief in God or an unwavering belief in oneself, should drive me forward in doing everything I could to preserve my life.

She told me of her mother, and her sister, and how their bodies were ravaged by illness as they each emerged into their late fifties and early sixties, but how, despite the pain of treatments, regardless of the impossible, each fought to sustain, fought to champion over their illnesses.

Fought to live.

This was not a removed observance for me, as I remembered as a little girl and into my teens the struggles and battles Aunt Marie, Grandmom Philly's sister, endured as a woman with chronic kidney disease. She lived only through the miracle of dialysis, which became a part of her life in the 1970s, administered by doctors and nurses pushing kidney care to its limits to squeeze more months into her lifetime.

I think some of the techniques Aunt Marie endured were even journaled by her physicians. I remember the thickness and hardness of the shunt placed in her arm so she could receive her dialysis treatments. I remember the stories, that her dialysis shunt was made of a bovine graft, and she was one of the first kidney patients in South Philadelphia to get one.

Aunt Marie, the Rita Hayworth of Mifflin Street, with bovine in her arm.

The pills. The procedures. The endurance of being connected to dialysis machines three times a week, an effort supported by medical transport vehicles to and from her home. Her years of commuting to dialysis, with each year taking its toll with weight loss, exhaustion, nausea, pain, confusion, even, at times, despair. The support of her husband, Uncle Mikey, to watch her endure her own war her body was waging against her, as he fought the demons that came home with him from his coming of age on the battlefields of France in World War II.

And yet, in prepping for her dialysis duties, my Aunt Marie would brush her hair back, put on red lipstick, flirt with

Uncle Mikey as they waited for the medical transport vehicle to pick her up to take her to her doctors and nurse and her dialysis machine. Her hair, damaged from the cruel fragility of disease, still combed meticulously. Her lipstick applied with expert strokes and primping.

She felt like absolute death, drained and pitifully empty, yet, when she put all her energy into going to dialysis, this small woman, enduring the failing of her body, was still the Rita Hayworth of Mifflin Street. She was convinced most of her doctors were secretly in love with her.

They probably were.

In the end, after she endured over a decade of dialysis and, she pushed into her 65th year, at which point she was released of her body's weaknesses on a rainy June afternoon. Her flaming red lipstick would no longer grace her lips. She had driven her last mile to dialysis.

Drifting into the memories of all who loved her, most of all my Grandmom Philly, Aunt Marie was eternally free. She was forever the Rita Hayworth of Mifflin Street; the bovine graft only made her more legendary. She never gave up, nor did she diminish.

She was a star, all on her own.

"Sometimes," my Grandmom Philly said as we huddled together along the wooded path, which now seemed to be chilling off with an unusually bitter breeze. "Sometimes, it is as simple as taking one day to the next. Believe you can get through today. Then do it. Then get through tomorrow. Then you get through the next day. If you don't dwell on the outcome, or what the outcome might be, you just go forward."

"I am going forward," I assured her. "Just because I'm tired, doesn't mean I'm finished."

"Good, because it is just not your time. Your Aunt Marie never thought how much time she had, or what five weeks ahead were going to be – she only thought about her todays. This is what I, what we all want for you Penny, we want you to focus on your todays," Grandmom Philly said.

I could feel my eyes filling with warm tears. I sank into her words and allowed myself to feel the safety and protection of her spirit. She took a few more steps with me, then stopped just short of a bend in the pathway ahead. Leaning against me, she squeezed my hands and gestured forward, nodding her head slowly giving me one final instruction – one last grandmotherly directive.

Her eyes were on mine.

*You need to go forward **without me now.***

Looking pensively ahead, I could see the bend of twigs, dirt and gravel obscured, virtually concealed, any hint of a structured path ahead. The trail seemed shadowed, an almost vivid cool filter coating the dirt, bushes, and trees, making the landscape ahead seem somehow shuddersome, not quite frightful, but cold sober.

Whatever was forward, was not Mifflin Street.

"You know," she said as we walked further the increasingly frosty wooded trail. "I had my own walk, but for me, it was when I was a girl."

A deliberate chill was suddenly everywhere.

"When you were a girl, what do you mean," I asked her, wondering what the rules and parameters were for this experience. Certainly, if she had her walk experience as a girl, it could not have been an end-of-life encounter, but then, what was it if not an experience that one has when on the verge of a transition – from life to death, from the past to a future unknown.

"You're thinking too much," she told me.

Did she know my thoughts?

"You are walking with your brain too much with this Penny – you have to just go through it, walk with your heart. It doesn't make sense, I don't think it's supposed to but when you are finished, when this is done, it will make sense for you. It will Penny, I promise you. You'll figure it out, then you'll go home to your kids, and you'll keep being who you need to be."

Who I needed to be. Do we ever stop being who we need to be? Grandmom Philly was who I needed her to be right now, and she's dead. What if ....

"Will you stop already," she told me. "You have to listen, not think."

As we took our steps together, arm in arm, the weight of her leaning on me increasing as the walk took more of her energy, she told me the story of her brother, Louis. I already knew of Louis, of course, as she told me of him before many times. How he was born afflicted, weak and with a body unable to walk, hands unable to clasp. I remember the only picture I ever saw of Louis, maybe the only picture ever taken of him, showed a boy, by the

Mifflin Street house's front steps, maybe six or seven, sitting in a wooden wheelchair of the early 1900s design, with large, swooping wheels and a seat that looked more like an intricately woven basket. The basket cradled him, his thin legs held up by the wood of the chair, while his tiny arms were pressed against his torso, with his hands held like fists against him. Still, his face was serene, his hair straight and I would see his features were like those of my grandmother – he was a beautiful, weak boy, burdened by the weight of an illness that would limit his life until it took it entirely.

By the time my Grandmom Philly was emerging from her toddler years into her girlhood, she too encountered grave illness, not one menacingly graced upon her at birth, but one incurred. By this time, Louis was gone, his mortal struggles lifted from him, or him from them.

"I was so sick, my mother, everyone, they didn't know if I would live. My fevers were high, my body would shake, and sweat. Oh, it was terrible. Terrible for my poor mother. My mother would never leave my side, she would sleep at the foot of my bed, and she was sleeping right there one night, my feet were her pillow, when I saw him," Grandmom Philly told me.

"He was just outside the bedroom door, in the black, black hallway. And he …. *glowed*."

Grandmom Philly went on to tell me more of her vision of Louis, his smile warm, his face joyous and his small body framed in a shimmering glow that garmented him in sunbeams. It was this vision of Louis, aglow in a pitch-black hallway, that stayed strong in her heart and mind over the many decades she would live beyond her childhood illness.

Louis…

"He came to me, he didn't talk to me, but he smiled at me and reached for me to join him in the hallway. Somehow, I did – and when I touched his hand, he took me on my walk."

Grandmom Philly told me of the places she saw while on her adventure with Louis.

The churches.

The houses.

The ocean.

The pathways filled with flowers.

She was transported, or perhaps returned, to the land of her people – of her heart.

Calabria. With her big brother, she walked the paths around the Southern Italian peninsula, by the Cattolica di Stilo church, stopping to touch the walls of it as it stood steadfast in time. They walked the cradle of what was once the migration of Greeks into the tip of the boot of Italy, bordered by the Ionian Sea and the Tyrrhenian Sea, with sunbaked coastlines famous of Reggio Calabria, the very land over which thousands of Greek warriors marched in antiquity. This was the land of her ancestors, generations of people occupying Greek lands, migrating into the Italian hillsides, bringing celery things variations with them. It was an adventure for Louis and Grandmom Philly. Walking the land of their family's history, until their pathway led them to a small home beyond the borders of Reggio Calabria, near the panoramic seaside leading west to the breezes of the Tyrrhenian. Their steps were inches and miles at the same time.

The little home that called to them was modest. It was the home her father had grown up in, and it was still very much alive.

"I saw my father's mother, she hugged me, and Louis, and she told me I was going to be better. She told me I was going to be strong again," Grandmom Philly told me. "She told me this while sitting on her rocking chair on the porch of her house in Calabria. The house where she was born. She told me stories of her childhood, of her mother, of raising her own sons in that same little house, of her grandfather's devotion to the sea, where he lost his life. She told me of her lifetime. She spoke to me in Italian, and though I only knew some Italian, I understood her. Every word, I understood. I could see Louis understood her too. I think Louis spends time with her a lot."

She spoke her father's mother's words to me.

Sei qui perché sei ovunque. Sei ovunque per sempre. Non avere paura.

Translated, the meaning is roughly:

You are here because you are everywhere. You are everywhere forever. Have no fear."

"That's so amazing, she told you to have no fear. She wanted you to know you would get through that time," I said to her. "She was the star of your walk, yes? Your ... *Walk Day?*"

"Well, your grandfather likes to call these *Walk Days*, and I guess that one was mine. I think Louis was the real star. Your Grandpop thinks walks happen all the time, sometimes it is to give you hope, that's how it was for me and your Aunt Elvira, hers was a lot like mine. She went to Calabria too, and only saw two or three people, including me – or so she says – as a baby."

Our steps quickened as she continued.

"For some people, and Penny, I think you are one of them, the experience can be bigger. More people. More voices. *More*. Your grandfather's walk, my gosh, it was long. He was with his mother, and he saw many people. Everyone experiences something different, and only when they need it the most. That's what I think anyway," Grandmom Philly told me. "Some people, they get no walk at all. I don't know why, either they don't deserve one, or they don't believe in what they see at the start enough to take the walk. I don't know. We talk about that a lot, why some don't get a walk. Or don't want one? Aunt Elvira thinks they don't deserve one, but I think she's wrong."

As we took more steps together, Grandmom Philly seemed to pick up her step.

I walked with astonishment and an escalating feeling of reluctance to continue. We continued together, with a bit more haste, and in each quickened step we filled the air with stories of my kids, and her questions about my life in the years she missed. We talked about my son's wedding, my oldest daughter's graduation from medical school. We talked about the births of all of my kids. I let her know how much my youngest reminds me of her, with the same soft, sweeping waves of black hair framing interested, empathetic eyes. We talked about celery things.

We talked about my Dad.

We cried about my Mom.

I filled her in on my brother's life in Portland, of his success in building his life on the West Coast. With each bit of information, she voiced her approval, pushed questions, and gave her opinions. It felt just like when I would sit on the edge of her bed, catching up with her. She reminded me of her secret to the best tasting meatballs. I had to tell her all her favorite afternoon soaps were off the air. I showed her my cell phone, which was not working.

We laughed about the time she fell off the steps at our cousin Joe's house, giving her a scar on her left shoulder, which she gleefully told me was no longer there. She told me of her latest feud with one of her sister-in-laws, not Grandpop Tony's youngest sister, Mary, they were on good terms. We talked about her dog, Lady, who died when I was a little girl, but who Grandmom Philly assured me was sleeping upstairs on a bed at the Mifflin Street house during my visit. She told me about her dinners with Aunt Margaret and Uncle Jimmy, Aunt Carrie and Uncle Johnny and other couples and friends from her generation, aunts, uncles, cousins and more, when they come over to play cards and enjoy the vibrantly full void of whatever this place is together.

We talked about how much things have changed at my parents' house. Renovations and upgrades over the years. How the room that was once hers there is now a sitting room., with a blue loveseat comfy with oversized white pillows. She told me to take a look at the bags of blankets she knitted decades ago, tucked under the stairwell closet at my parents' home. She reminded me there are blankets tucked away I could really be using, and them sitting in plastic bags are doing nothing for anybody but taking up space. We spent at least 20 minutes talking about Michael, his life, his divorce, his home, his motorcycles, his pension, his amazing son, his health, his concerns, his hobbies – anything I could think to share about Michael.

Michael was always her favorite.

Walking with her, toward what I did not know, or even care, felt like a release of all that weighted and pressured me. I no longer felt too small for my troubles. I felt just the right size to manage what I needed to manage. I felt distracted, and focused, at the same time. I felt connected to my family, and strong enough to stand on my own. I felt engaged and immersed, in my place in life, what I mean to the people I can no longer see, and what I mean to those who see me as they need me to be in their lives. I felt substantially more able-bodied, and capable.

I felt more like me.

"It's getting colder, do you feel it?" Grandmom Philly asked.

I could feel it.

We stopped.

I could see that, down the wooded trail, in all its greenery that is Acadia National Park in August, despite the shades of green that swayed on the treetops, despite the fresh blades of green grass bordering our earthy pathway, despite all that made sense – the cause of the penetrating chill presented itself. The wintry air. The nipping breezes. The tightening feel of winter on my shoulders, despite the fact that it was August.

It was now making sense.

Almost.

It was snowing.

"Is that ... what is *that*?" I asked Grandmom Philly.

"That's the end of our walk," she said, smiling at me, and giving my arm an extra hard clutching. "You go on now. I won't ever be too far from where you are," she told me. "I have to get back to the house now, I'm tired and I'm sure Aunt Elvira is wondering what's taking me so long."

The familiarity of this moment hit me. This moment of parting – this goodbye *sensation* with my grandmother. I more fully understood the feeling of reluctance taking over me earlier.

When I was 31, I had to say goodbye to Grandmom Philly.

One of the last visits we had, she and I were sitting on her bed in the nursing facility her health had landed her in during the final year of her life. Though she would come to my parents' home for days at a time for visits, due to her medications and other health needs, and the fact that, at that time, she would have been alone in the house for too many hours each day, the difficult choice for her to settle into a nursing facility was made by all, including her. This was a choice made with not a little disappointment and regret, though everyone tried to make the best of it.

Especially Grandmom Philly.

Still, on one of our last visits together, we talked in very final terms. I don't know why. Our conversations were never too deep, mostly on the goings on of the family, what's new in the world, updates on my kids, my job, joking about something, reminiscing about everything, but in the moments of reality that cracked into our conversations in our final visits together, we both knew a truth. Our visits were numbered.

With each visit, with each silly or heartfelt or even argumentative conversation, the moment was inching ever closer to what would be our last words.

Our last conversation was a good one.

I told her, as we laughed about too many years of memories to recount, that I did not know what I would do without her? She flatly knew what to tell me. "You will be fine; you have your baby to raise (*my oldest at the time was barely two*) and you have a lot to do for a long time – you will be alright."

"But" I replied to her with an escalating lump in my throat. "I will miss you."

"I'm going to miss you too, Penny," said told me, her own words chunking out in lumpy pauses.

And with that both of us found that our eyes were less dry, as we took in that moment, each of us letting the reality of our words soak in and each of us, in our own ways, already missing the other. She died not long after that conversation.

And I missed her.

Nevertheless, as she told me, I was alright. This was the moment that flipped fast to the front of my mind as I found myself getting ready to miss her all over again. She must have remembered it too. Looking straight into my eyes, she took a step back, extending her arms to support me. She smiled at me and told me not to fear anything. "You're a smart girl, you know anything you see today is all for you, it's always all for you. We are all walking with you today, you have us – what a lucky girl you are."

She continued to step away from me, gesturing with a tilt up of her chin for me to go forward.

"I love you Grandmom," I said to her, as I steadied myself to go on without her.

"I know you do, I love you too, Penny," she said to me in return and, as she uttered her goodbye I could see the path a few feet behind her begin to glow a sunbeam hue as the dirt began to vibrate with pops of gleaming, golden particles slowly drifting up from the ground, illuminating the trees and bushes and giving my grandmother a radiance that framed her in a dazzling effulgence of sunbeams.

The path nearest to her came alive with vibrant golden waves of sunlight that stretched and reached out for her to walk over them. The woods were aglow with iridescent washes of honey and caramel, which washed Grandmom Philly in otherworldly beauty.

She was unearthly, and even dead, yet my grandmother.

"Think about your todays Penny, think of all your todays," she told me, as she stepped deeper into the waves of sunbeams. I could see she was, with each step, casting a loving expression my way, as her face was aglow, I could see she again looked decades younger and, with that, her smiling expression drifted into the gleaming, lustrous pillars of gold that now seemed to carry her away. I still felt her presence, as if she continued, somehow, to stand next to me on the phantom trail, tucked in an unknown corner of lost time in Maine.

"What's easy losing is not worth having," I said to the air. "I know you can hear me, Girl."

As I spoke to the air, the faint sound of my grandmother calling out for Michael rode the breeze. I pictured her back at the Mifflin Street house, maybe clearing away the dinner plates, arguing with Aunt Marie and trying to get little Michael to stop throwing himself down the stairs and stomping all around the house.

She would not be successful, I bet.

The Hammering

I felt extremely tired. The chilly path I walked was the opposite of the ethereal golden path that appeared for my walk with Grandmom Philly. The path I was on now was earthy, very gritty, and very, very frigid. It was almost monochrome. I could hear the dirt crunching under my feet.

As I walked with unfluctuating consistency, the beats of my feet on the gravel and dirt were almost hypnotizing. Monotonous. Immutable. Unvarying. The uniformity of my footsteps became like an invisible companion to me. Unbroken and regular, the shuffling and grinding of the dirt beneath my feet served as an unalterable partner, even protector.

I was not alone.

Until my feet stopped.

Whether the emotional exhaustion of the experience, the absolute confusion of the day, or the longing I had to go back for more celery things soup, I stopped. My backpack felt heavy. My accomplice in this leg of my journey was silent, as my feet rested, firmly planted in the light snow that escorted my trip down this new and solitary path. My muddled mind was lost in thoughts.

What time is it?

Is there time anymore?

Was any of this real?

Was I in some medication-induced hallucination?

What if all of this is the afterlife?

What if I'm dead?

Why is it snowing?

Then, I heard it.

Again.

Ting, ting, ting.

Ting, ting, ting.

Fading in and out of the slowly shifting leaves, the bushes pushing in against the trail, I heard the comforting notes that, to me, meant only that my Sammie was once again nearby.

Ting, ting, ting.

Ting, ting, ting.

I looked down the path, speckled with a white dusting of fresh snow. The more I looked, the thicker the snow dusting grew and, as I approached it, I could see the unmistakable paw prints of a dog emerge in the white flakes, almost cookie cutter doggie paw prints peeking out from the doughy ground. Before long, I realized Sammie's paw prints encircled me, little silvery traces in the snow and dirt, signs of a hyper dog that was too magical to be real, and too real to be silent.

Ting, ting, ting.

Ting, ting, ting,

Ting, ting, tingling, tingling, ting, ting, ting, ting, tingling, ting.

The tingling sounds of her collar where everywhere and nowhere, lightly moving on the sobering breeze that whispered over my cheeks and, at the same time, gently nudged me to take my next steps. As I put my own footprints in the dusty white that now covered the Maine trail, I moved beyond a bend, around an enormous tree, and at that point heard what could only be described as a thundering, clapping sound. The closer I came to the sound, the more I understood its origins. It was hammering. Unmistakably hammering. A few more minutes on the trail, with the lulling consistency of the hammering in motion with my steps, I began to see the source of the noise.

It was a sight reminiscent of the nostalgic warmth brought to life by New England's famous storytelling illustrator, Norman Rockwell. How appropriate that I would encounter this New England sight while on a lonely stretch of Maine trail, not quite abandoned, occupied only by the unimaginable, or rather, the eternal.

Occupied only by the eternal.

And me.

And ... him.

Before me, I saw a man, who looked to be in his late 40s, kneeling on one knee as he hammered what appeared to be the finishing nails to a petite wooden table. The man wore a woven blue and white coat, that fit him a little too tightly across his broad shoulders. His hair looked to be very tight against his head, though the blue plaid winter cap with fur ears was all I could focus on as I watched him continue his assembly of the tiny table. His winter cap was a testament to textured tweed, its blue plaid dotted with the same white dust that lined the dirt trail. The same white dust that seemed to now be gently drifting around me, landing on my shoulders, my hands, my face.

It was not until the white dust touched my face that I actually believed it was snow.

"Can you hand me that nail," the man called out to me, his booming voice rattled the air. He lifted his head away from his work and at that point, seeing his face, that strong jawline, those thick eyebrows that almost mirrored the fur of his winter cap, the softness of his eyes, the felicity of his gaze.

I recognized the man.

I knew exactly who was next on my walk.

"Penny, I'm almost finished, come hand me that nail please, it rolled away," he said to me. It was my mother's father, my Pop Pop, strong and stolid and, even though he passed away at the age of 78 when I was in my teens, apparently, in this moment, very much alive, in sturdy health and by all accounts, busy.

He reached out his left hand for me to place the wayward nail into his glove.

So much rushed into my mind.

Why didn't Grandmom Philly give me an idea of who I would meet? Why didn't I think to ask?

I found myself just peering at Pop Pop, as you would a Norman Rockwell you had never seen before – taking in the familiar hints of loving nostalgia while exploring the lines and contours of a uniquely new sight. The way his eyebrows pushed together when annoyed, the crinkle his mouth made when his patience was ticking away, the commanding way his neck would jerk back a bit, in disbelief of what he was, himself seeing.

This is unquestionably my grandfather, but what does this all ....

"Penny!" Pop Pop called out, with a slight push of impatience. "I know you are turning over in your head, this and that, and we'll get to all that, but come on now, the nail. I'm almost finished. This is for your mother. I have to get this done tonight, it's Christmas Eve. I'm only a few more nails away from done. Once I finish this up, you and I can talk about why you are here. Now, get that nail."

And with that, I took three steps closer to him, noticed the lost nail glistening in the snow, picked it up and placed it in the middle of his gloved hand. He smiled at me, closing his hand around the glove, gently moving his hand a bit as if to savor the recovery of the nail and, a moment later, the hammer was back at work – my mother's miniature Christmas Eve table was complete.

"Praise God, that's a relief, she only told us she wanted a table and chairs tonight. This here, right here, it's a Christmas miracle," he said, getting up from his kneeling position and gesturing behind him for me to see two tiny chairs, which were fashioned to match the diminutive table.

Each chair had little flowers carved into the seats, one a bit rudimentary, but given that they were built fast I was impressed with the detail.

I also recognized the table – as I grew up seeing it in our garage. A bit worse for wear by the time I came to know it, with years of standing strong for afternoon tea parties, countless crayon and watercolor drenched creations, a curious history of chocolate milk spills, and, in its later life, shouldering the burden of holding up boxes of books and photo albums. The table still existed, tucked in my parents' garage as its builder stood before me. The chairs, as cute as they were, made with his rushed, loving hands, did not stand the test of time as well as did the table.

I was not going to share that fact with my Pop Pop.

"When your mother told your Mom Mom and I that all she wanted for Christmas was a table and chairs from Santa, I knew it was going to be a long night," he said, laughing, his deep voice giving a vibrant lift to the cold air. "Thanks for your help, I couldn't have finished it without you. Now, let's get to why you are here. It seems we have some building of our own to do together, doesn't it Penny?"

And with that, he effortlessly hoisted my mother's new table over his strong right shoulder.

And we began our walk.

He gestured for me to pick up the two miniature chairs he had fashioned, as they were small and light, I had no trouble with the task, despite my backpack now firmly etched into my right side. Despite the long walk to get to Pop Pop, despite the chill of the air, I felt that resurgence again, a push of youthful power and vitality. I felt animated, and, once again, as I had experienced on Mifflin Street, I noticed my hair was, again, longer, thick waves and curls down the front of me. My feet felt as though I had not walked even a step, and my shoulders seemed to push back, giving me the extra potency needed to lift the tiny chairs and fall in step with Pop Pop. My clothes, again, felt baggy and stretched. I could see my fingers were lean, and the skin covering them was angelic. Not a line. Not a wrinkle. Not a scratch. Not a hint of five decades of service.

Does he see me as I am, or does he see me as he thinks I am? Am I what he thinks I am? Hold old does he think I am?

"Here we go Penny, let's get on," Pop Pop told me, starting his motion down the pathway.

With the table on his shoulder, and my mother's little chairs in my arms, we began to make footprints in the light snow, side by side, as we walked together. I couldn't see Sammie paw prints anymore, nor hear her ting, ting, tingling, but I sensed she was just out of reach, beyond the treelined trail. Maybe she was taking a nap now that she saw I was in good hands.

Thank you, Sammie, you're such a good girl.

As the crunching sound of my walk over gravel and dirt commenced, I asked my grandfather.

"Where are we going, Pop Pop?"

"We're going home Penny," he told me. "Cedar Avenue, where else?"

Pop Pop

When he was born in May of 1904, Pop Pop's family lived in the coal mining mountains of Tamaqua, Pennsylvania, before moving to the suburbs of Philadelphia, where they resided on a farm that was once a British encampment during the Revolutionary War. While there, Pop Pop's father worked as a blacksmith for the farm's owners, a prosperous Pennsylvania family with roads, stores, and schools branded in their honor.

The first time my Pop Pop saw his home on Cedar Avenue in Upland, Pennsylvania, he was emerging from boy to man. He would tell stories of walking to the Cedar Avenue house for the first time the year the house was built on Upland soil in 1918, leaving the British encampment for a two-story, three-bedroom house that would be his family's own, and situated closer to his father's new employment at a steel mill. The house sat on a steep hill, near the middle of the street and on a large corner created when Upland changed its mind about running a street through what ended up being the house's west side and ample backyard.

Tucked between Church Street and Main Street, all built on what was once a tobacco plantation settled sometime in the 1600s between the Chester Creek and Ridley Creek, flowing to the Delaware River, Pop Pop's Cedar Avenue house sat on soil rich in the pain of abandonment.

The town's original settlers were Swedish, calling the land *Oplandt*, which became Upland. The Lenni Lenape Tribe were Upland's original inhabitants but, as the migration of Swedes, Finns and more pushed into the Chester Creek region, the land was colonized, erasing the legacy of its true people almost entirely. William Penn himself frequently visited Upland, staying at the Caleb Pusey house, where he shared his intent with the community to provide vital infrastructure for landowners, and scores of incoming European explorers and settlers, not to mention Quakers and other religious minorities.

The displacement of the Lenni Lenape from Upland was calculated and tragic.

Commanding the land destined to be Philadelphia, its surrounding territories and much of the southern region of New Jersey, the Lenni Lenape cherished their rolling hills, forests of green pine, evergreen, chestnut, walnut, oak, and hickory trees. They honored the land's moss, meadows, berries, mushrooms, strawberries, and the corn that grew wild in fields of gold. As time pushed forward, fading into history were the dome-shaped, single-doorway wooden wigwams of the Lenni Lenape. By 1682, William Penn entered into purchase agreements with the Lenni Lenape that resulted in vast lands deeded away from their original inhabitants. By 1737, the Lenni Lenape lost all claims to the terrain that had been of their bones for centuries. A few more years beyond that point, Pennsylvania colonial officials called on the Iroquois to push any remaining Lenni Lenape out entirely.

The Lenni Lenape were forced to abandon Upland.

Pop Pop's father would do the same, willingly.

Pop Pop's first arrival at the Cedar Avenue house must have looked like a scene out of a movie, at least that's how I picture it.

A dusty roadway.

Horses on the ready.

A barefoot trek.

Pop Pop's father, an Irish coal miner turned steelworker, mother and two little sisters rode in a hay wagon piled high with furniture and all their belongings. At a strong age of 14, Pop Pop walked alongside the wagon, carrying large wooden chip baskets made out of splits of firewood. Everything the family had in the world, from mattresses to pots and pans to baskets of bread baked the day before the big move, to wooden chests filled with handmade shirts and trousers stitched by Pop Pop's mother and grandmother, everything was in the hay wagon. It overflowed with chair legs hanging out like branches and loaded up baskets of various sizes, secured with twine. His mother's mother, Bridget Tammany, lived with the family, all journeying to the Cedar Avenue home that would serve as the family's final encampment.

A father, a mother, three kids, one very Irish grandmother, and an overstocked hay wagon.

My Pop Pop's father would not settle at Cedar Avenue for long.

Pop Pop's father grew up with the weight of emptiness on his shoulders, having been neglected, later abandoned, by his mother and, eventually, delivered to his grandparents by his father. Family lore would tell the story of Pop Pop's father, as a boy, following his mother as she walked down a dirt road away from their home, turning around only to throw stones at him, screaming at him to stop following her. With his mother gone, his father did the only thing he could think to do for his son. He put Pop Pop's father on a train and told the boy where to get off.

The *where* would lead him to his grandparents, who would give him a roof, meals, and care.

The *where* would not fill the emptiness that overtook him.

He, like his mother, and father, would abandon his own family, forced out of Upland, not by unsurmountable external combatants, but by undeniable internal conflicts. Some say he tried, working numerous jobs, helping to raise his three children. Until, one day, he stopped trying. Whether it was premeditated, or a shock, even to him, the day came that served as his last day as a husband and a father. He walked away from the family's Cedar Avenue house, and into the fog of generational gossip, legendary for the void that he left when his tendencies to follow the footsteps of his mother overtook him.

Maybe he was always the boy following his mother down that dirt road.

From one father to the next, a legacy of abandoning their families. These were the men that my Pop Pop descended from, a legacy of abandonment and emptiness born from the disappointments of generations that, despite best efforts, were unable to divorce themselves from their destinies – to disappoint, to despair, to disappear.

My Pop Pop did not disappear.

Unlike his own father, and his father's father, my Pop Pop was inherently dutiful, with a lifetime of devotion to his family, his community, and his God. Even in his boyhood, he spirited a life of service and support for all those who needed him, whether family, neighbor, friend or even enemy. Pop Pop, and the love of his life, my Mom Mom, isolated the family they made on Cedar Avenue, my mother, the youngest of three daughters, and one son. Theirs was a household of effortless respectability, contribution to community, endorsement of education, and devotion to the teachings of God. Theirs was a household, not devoid of struggles, but strong enough to weather difficulties, to stand tall in despair and overcome. While the Cedar Avenue house may have seen the dissolution of Pop Pop's first family, his second family – the one he made – would flourish in its walls.

Cedar Avenue would not be deserted, not by my Pop Pop – a man of faith, a man of community, a man with the strength and character to create a legacy of family.

"I can't tell you how many times I walked this street with family, Penny," Pop Pop said to me as we walked briskly along the trail, etching our footprints in the snow with each step and shuffle, until the dirt under our feet turned to snow-dusted sidewalk, with little cracks and dents showing its longevity. As our footsteps brought us closer to our destination, Pop Pop began reminiscing about his mother, and how much she loved making molasses candy at Christmas.

I wondered if his mother was somewhere waiting for us. Maybe she was making molasses candy. I doubted his father was anywhere waiting for us, at least, I hoped he wasn't.

A few more steps, and we were there. Emerging from the snow-covered bushes and treetops, it was my mother's childhood home. The closer we got, the more the two-story Cedar Avenue house pushed out of the woods – until its entire front stood before us, the wooden porch, the rocking chairs set in motion with no one in them, a holiday wreath on the front door. Pop Pop thumped one foot, then the other, up the wooden steps onto the porch and set my mother's miniature table down. I followed suit, placing the petite chairs with the table.

"Take a seat Miss Penny," Pop Pop said, as the Cedar Avenue house took full form. With that, he plopped his body into a chair and leaned back, as if to remove an ache from his shoulders. I sat in the rocking chair next to him, and together, we motioned our chairs back and forth a bit, each of us resting from our walk – and each of us, it seemed, waiting for the other to put words between us.

I breathed in deeply.

The last time I saw my Pop Pop, I was a teenager, maybe 14 or 15. My parents and I visited him in the hospital. He was in good spirts and seemed as sturdy and strong as ever. My mother had decided she wanted to begin journaling his stories – which were plentiful, and entertaining.

Tales of people he knew, diverse, bold and even unbelievable characters from his life, the lore of his community, and the remarkable experiences that formed him – the good and the brutal. We had our hospital visit with him, my mother jotted a story or two he felt inclined to share, we marked the day golden and, though each of us were unaware of it, it would be the last time we would speak together. The next day, quite suddenly, as he brushed his teeth over the sink in his hospital room, he died. Within the span of less than 12 hours since we had seen him, his stories drifted away into the memories of those who had heard them over the many decades of his captivating storytelling. His robust vocabulary. His sharp observational humor. His decisive memory. His masterfully colorful descriptors.

The boisterous and booming tone of voice as he would bring his hefty tales to life. Silenced, as his toothbrush hit his hospital room floor. Yet, here he was, sitting within inches of me, motioning for me to say something. He raised his thick eyebrows at me and pointed at my mother's newly crafted table and chairs.

"What do you think, Miss Penny?" he asked me, with a grimace.

"I think you did a very good job," I told him, smiling back. "My mother told me about this, about asking Santa for the table and chairs, and how you stayed up all night one Christmas Eve making sure she would not be disappointed in the morning. That was one of her favorite memories of you."

"Well, that's good," Pop Pop confirmed. "Do you know *why* I wanted her to see a table and chairs that Christmas morning. True, Miss Penny, I did not want her to be disappointed, of course, but there was another reason why I had to make this table and chairs for her. Can you tell me what that reason was, and don't overthink it – I'm hearing that you are overthinking a lot today."

"Well," I told him, wondering who filled Pop Pop in on my earlier walk and talks. "I guess you wanted her to believe in Santa. The magic of Christmas? You didn't want her to feel like Santa didn't hear her, right? You wanted her to feel special, to feel loved."

He laughed.

Loudly.

A booming laugh that caused me to start laughing too. I hoped the wood porch could take the power of his laugh, because moments ago this porch wasn't even here and now, with each passing second, I felt a fragility of it sustaining us as Pop Pop just laughed and laughed.

"I'm sorry," he said, bringing his laughter to a gentle landing. "What's so funny for me, Miss Penny Lane (*he sometimes called me Penny Lane, I guess he could not let Grandpop Tony have all the naming rights*) is that not only are you right, but you have made my job today so much easier – and I was nervous to talk to you about things. I wanted to find the right words, the best way in the minutes I have with you, to get you to believe again – and thankfully, I can see you are getting it. I can see you are understanding why I am here with you right now. I'm relieved."

I had no idea what he was talking about.

"You mean ... *Santa*? The magic of Christmas?" I asked him.

"Not ... exactly," he said, leaning forward in his chair, and resting his elbows on his knees. "It's more a belief in the impossible. A belief in the possibility that what you wish for might be waiting for you. It's about a belief in the magic of you – that magic that is within you, within all of us, and given to us every day of our lives, if we are open to receiving it and recognizing it."

"So, it's about, believing?" I asked him.

He smiled at me, nodding his head, but wrinkling his nose just a bit, signaling to me that I may not be getting the full message.

"Believing in getting what you hope for, what you wish for," I elaborated. "About closing your eyes and making a wish and believing that somehow, in some way, that wish comes true?"

He smiled again.

"Well, Penny, I think it's less about wishing," Pop Pop said. "It's about knowing that what you hope may come to you, will come to you. It's about believing, but more than that, it's about having faith. Believing in faith. Believing in strength. Believing you can endure and move forward, no matter what your circumstances might be. Believing in the power of your convictions, of your decisions, of your choices in life. It's about believing that you are a person of faith, and truly being one."

I do not think I ever knew a man with more faith than Pop Pop. It's too bad his father didn't have even a quarter of the faith Pop Pop carried.

I remembered my mother sharing stories of how Pop Pop never missed a Sunday Mass, and of how religiously he would light candles in their Cedar Avenue home in prayer, particularly after his mother died, how he would faithfully burn remembrance candles for her and keep them burning throughout the night. At times, the flame from the candles, usually placed on a narrow table in the upstairs hallway, would create dancing shadows on the hallway walls, entertaining my mother as she drifted off to sleep, only to discover, in the morning, the candles had decorated the hallway wall with modest blackened markings, charring the blue paint.

Candles and all, Pop Pop was a good son.

He bought the Cedar Avenue house from his mother, lovingly known as *Granny*, when his own family began to grow, and Granny, a person of faith herself, was a fixture within its rooms until the day she died. Devoted to her son, and his family, and her daughters and their families, Granny's strength of character and resilience guided her son forward, setting right the wrongs of his father – or at least, casting them out. Her talents as a seamstress would keep the roof over her family's head after Pop Pop's father abandoned the lot of them. Her penny pinching, her tenacity, her prayers. It was his mother's endurance and belief in the strength within her to lead her family that nourished life at Cedar Avenue.

It was his mother's love that broke the cycle of paternal abandonment that plagued Pop Pop's father and grandfather. It was her love that made Pop Pop a father who would stay to raise his children, a father who would build a table and chairs for his little girl's Christmas Eve tea party dreams. It was her faith that turned Cedar Avenue from a house to a home. It was in this moment, sitting with Pop Pop on the porch of his home, in the middle of a frozen patch of Maine wooded trail, in August, looking at the childhood table and chairs of my mother's Christmas dreams, I could feel within me a rising truth.

I was a person of faith too. I was a person who could endure, who could find strength ... *who could believe.*

Pop Pop began to smile at me again. This time, his smile was relaxed and slow, as if his body warmed as his lips pushed from ear to ear. His shoulders dropped to a comfortable placement, and it seemed as though he allowed himself to drift back in his rocking chair, just enough to catch a small nap in the time it took him to motion back and forth in the chair a few times. He was very much at ease, like an actor who had delivered his lines, received a standing ovation, and realized his performance mattered.

With his burly exterior and abundantly masculine persona, you'd be hard pressed to believe he could be tender and introspective, but to assume otherwise would be a great neglect. I think I always knew that about him, but in this isolated experience, sitting with him in this oddly placed fragment of time and space, I was reminded.

Pop Pop was a sweetheart.

"Isn't it wonderful to believe in all things good – to have faith when one feels faithless," Pop Pop said to me, giving my hands a slight squeeze as if to punctuate his message. "Life will always bring challenges; it will always feed on weaknesses – there will always be the unrelenting temptation to lose faith. There will always be the pull to give up. That's why it's so important, no matter what, to believe in the magic of what is possible, to wish and hope for good things. That's why, for you Miss Penny Lane, it's important to nourish your faith in all the good things that are still possible for you in life."

Pop Pop paused, looked out at the sky and the falling snow around us, and winked at me. "Belief is powerful, Penny. Faith is powerful," Pop Pop said, leaning closer to me as he whispered, his voice lowering as if to share with me a secret. "Faith is magic, Miss Penny."

As his voice carried those words toward me, I could feel a change in the air.

A Change in the Air

The crispness of this surprisingly wintery mix began creeping into the trees and, with that, my Pop Pop stood up, removed his thick winter jacket, plopped it on the wooden boards of the porch and opened his arms to me. I could see strokes of thin sunbeams begin popping through breaks in the tree canopy and, with the glow of the sun warming us, I knew my time with Pop Pop, on the porch of my mother's childhood house in Upland, was fading. I stepped forward and hugged my Pop Pop. He touched my chin, putting the tip of his index finger in the cleft of my chin, a trait that I think he felt I inherited from him, and, with that, he motioned me down the two steps, and back onto the dirt path which was now devoid of any snowflake remnants.

"I'm going to take this table and chairs inside now, and set them up for your mother," he told me, winking as he picked up the table and moved toward his front door. "You go on, you're not done yet today. You go on, you're not done yet today. Keep walking, the trail knows where you need to go."

I lifted my right hand and held it up as a combination of a wave and, in some ways, a longing, resolute outreach, almost a salute to this great man of strength and faith – a gesture of gratitude to a man who, in life, I knew just enough to admire, but not enough to miss him truly and deeply.

Until this moment.

I watched from the dirt trail as he carried my mother's tiny table into his house. I could see the Christmas tree lit up in the living room, but the rest of the house, it seemed, was sleeping. He stepped out onto his porch, lifted the two little chairs with each hand, smiled at me and, with that, went into the house, gently closing the front door behind him.

The glow from inside the house soaked the front porch in warmth and, subtle at first, I detected an overwhelmingly enticing scent. It was a cake baking, or something warm, sweet, and delicious being lovingly created. The air was filled with notes of brown sugar, molasses, or corn syrup. I wasn't sure exactly. Was I taking in the richness of dark raisins or pitted prunes, the hearty accents of both seemed to fill the air, mixed with the richness of strong coffee. I thought I even detected a hint of apples. Or was that nutmeg? My mother had always shared stories of her mother's baking. Cakes and pies, delicious and fresh, always filled her home when she was a girl.

My grandmother, Mom Mom, was an excellent cook, and an even better baker. One cake my mother would talk about was the Depression cake my grandmother would make, which often had no or very little milk, sugar, butter or even eggs. My mother, being the youngest, by far in her family, came at a time when her household had emerged out of the Great Depression, preparing to thrive into better days. Still, Mom Mom made good use of her ingredient substitutions, sometimes boiling raisins with a little syrup to bring sweetness to the practicality of the recipe.

Depression cakes brought a cheerful treat to homes existing on budgets so small feeding families was an art – and an effort. When Mom Mom and Pop Pop got married, the Stock Market Crash of 1929 was only a few months away. Young and in love, they eloped to Elkton, Maryland, to begin their lives together in February of 1929. They shocked their families, waiting for them nervously in their Upland, Pennsylvania, but, clearly in love, and with the help of time, all shocks subsided. The young couple went on to have a son, then two daughters and, when the youngest of their three children celebrated her tenth birthday – the surprise of my mother's conception delivered the family of five to six.

How many Depression cakes did my Mom Mom bake for her children? How many Depression cakes did she bake once my mother joined the household? I wondered if my mother even realized the cakes she grew up eating were experiments in baking on a budget – on surviving a time when milk, sugar and eggs were luxuries. As my mother grew into her teens, Mom Mom would craft delicious butter cakes, creamy chocolate cakes and fruit-loaded pies. My mother remembers the melt-in-your-mouth classic pound cakes, fluffy with four key ingredients often lacking from Mom Mom's Depression cakes: butter, sugar, eggs, and flour, in abundance – especially fresh butter. They were typically made with one heaping cup of soft butter, two cups of sugar, three cups of flour and four farm fresh eggs. At times creativity, and resources, spiced things up with apples or other fruits to bring the flavors higher.

As I stood motionless, I gratefully took in the aroma of nutmeg, mixed with warm spices and the savory thickness of fresh raisins. The sweet freshness was in the air – it was everywhere. You could almost imagine savoring the light texture of the warm cake as it flaked into granular bits of candied, sticky, nectarous pastry goodness. I could almost taste the harmonious, plummy richness of the incorporated raisins mashing with the mellow, fruity traces of sugariness.

Mom Mom's Depression cakes must have tasted delicious.

I found myself wanting to stay, to walk through the front door and into the house – to see Mom Mom baking in the kitchen, probably complete with a 1950s floral housedress and white apron. To see my mother's mother in her element, baking in a warm kitchen, while Pop Pop placed the last of my mother's Christmas gifts under a fresh Christmas tree, adorned with homemade popcorn beading, woven ornaments and a few very carefully placed candles, would be a sight. What a wonderful Christmas morning my mother would awake to, with freshly baked treats and gifts waiting for her.

Just then, I realized the whiffs of warm apple and sweet raisin were, sadly, beginning to lessen. I took a few steps away from the house, but I kept my eyes on its front door. My time visiting the Upland house that raised my mother was inching into oblivion. I took a few slow steps away. I could see the first indications of what grew quickly to be glorious, meticulously cut sunbeams breaking out of the windows of the house like shimmering threads of magical yarn. Like the Mifflin Street house earlier, the Cedar Avenue house began to shimmer, with golden threads of light blurring into bursts of yellow radiance.

The wooden front porch began to crackle and bend, the boards seemingly folding in on themselves, retreating and receding, almost melting, into the tree-lined thickness of the Maine trail on which I found myself, once again, alone. As the last specs of the front porch disappeared into the twigs and brush, I could see sparks of gold popping like confetti everywhere the front porch, only moments ago, had occupied on the dirt trail.

With the last flicker of gold quieted, and all vestiges of the two-story house evaporated, I turned definitively toward the trail ahead of me – ready for my next encounter and armed with a resurgence of faith in myself, and in the miracle of the journey forward.

As I took my steps, I felt the ache of my lower back chime in, reminding me that my more youthful persona was once again replaced by the older, not quite fully wiser, version left to navigate the path ahead. Taking a few dozen steps, thick, heavenly notes of warm apples, surprisingly, filled the air again, as a sunny breeze touched my face. I relished in the sensation of being surrounded by warmth, the sweet scent of baked apples all around me.

It was no longer Christmas Eve.

But I still *believed*.

I took a few next steps and, as I made my way further down the trail, all detectable hints of ambrosial deliciousness echoed away. With every step, the trail, only moments ago redolent of sweet spices, was back to its naturally earthy scents. The freshness of the grass. A hint of dampness in the breeze. The almost undetectable fibrous composition of stems, branches, and slightly wet tree bark. The murky, sticky reminders of a sodden Maine trail in August.

Walking firmly on the dirt trail, feeling a bit hungry, I wondered how Mom Mom's Depression cake tasted and, although I would never sample it for myself, I believed it to be magnificent and, in that belief, I was satisfied.

"I will believe," I said to the wind as I walked over the gravel and dirt, the stones and dried leaf fragments furbishing the grooves of my route. Cedar Avenue had drifted back into the trees, back perhaps in time, certainly beyond the wooded coverage of Maine. My mother's childhood home, returned to its supernatural resting place, somewhere back in *Oplandt*.

A hint of warm, baked apples filled the air once again.

Where Am I?

When you are walking along a wooded trail alone, time molds itself around you.

My mind was filled with my day's walks, the surprising conversations of my time alone with everyone magically there to greet me in the beautiful expanse of Acadia National Park.

Grandpop Tony.

Aunt Elvira.

Grandmom Philly.

Pop Pop.

Was I walking for 10 minutes or two hours? There was no hint of what was coming next. Would I be back on Mifflin Street? Is Cedar Avenue gone forever? Will I see my husband? Will I see my Grandpop Tony again, before all this is over? What can I expect next? Where are my clues? Why haven't I seen my husband yet? Is he not going to be a part of my Walk Day? I mean, it's my birthday too?

Why would he miss today?

I found myself getting annoyed.

No piercing sunbeams.

No hint of warm apples.

No snowflakes.

No ting, ting, tingling.

The trail was very much just ... a trail.

All I could feel was this timeless sensation of being utterly swallowed up by the environment that surrounded me, fallen into a place in time, separate from any fixed location, or era of my lifetime. How old am I? Where would this trail take me? Is this trail my final journey in life?

Is my life this trail, is this trail my life?

My father battled cancer in his early fifties, and again in his early sixties. He beat it. His father, my Grandpop Tony, had cancer in his sixties. It beat him. Now it was my turn. Days turned to weeks, then months, of living with cancer, following treatments, making every appointment set to battle for life, trying to be uplifting and cheery for my kids. After months and months of listening to test results, the cheeriness became real. I may be in remission. I may be dizzyingly, euphorically in remission. I feel terrible most of the time, but things are starting to look good. If this can only last, if I can sustain this trajectory. Maybe, I will beat my high-maintenance friend, if I believe hard enough.

I looked up from the ground, still walking, as my thoughts crashed over me like waves.

Wait, where am I?

Why am I not seeing anyone else?

Can I go back to Cedar Avenue?

What is that?

Is that laughing?

Who is laughing?

I stopped walking.

Intently, I turned my head, and, as if seeking signals from beyond, I listened.

Nothing.

Silence.

Then …

There it was again.

Laughter.

Looking to my right, motionless once again in anticipation of discovery, I saw the young woman responsible for gifting the warm August air with a gleeful laughter. I looked at her, she looked at me. She seemed only about 15 or 16, sparkling eyes, beautiful, full cheeks flush with the rose hue of youthful energy.

The pink gown she was wearing looked majestic, a blushing rose-colored gown, it could have been a bridesmaid dress or prom gown perhaps, with the fabric adorning her body, shimmering around her shoulders, and bunching up slightly around her waist, where an oversized blush rose bow tied her middle, making her look more like a present, than a person.

Her full upper arms were healthy, her red curls flowing over her shoulders framed her angelic expression. Her laughter was of the wind, everywhere – joyous, frolicsome, and vexatious. There was something wickedly provoking about her laugh. The kind of laughter that makes you want to laugh too, then get into trouble, then laugh about the trouble you got into.

She was young.

She was healthy.

She was real.

My cousin Peggy.

Always lively, even provocative at times, and never without the energy to bring disruptive humor to any family event. It didn't matter if it was a wedding or a funeral, a backyard birthday party or a Thanksgiving meal, Peggy would enthrall. She was unarguably enchanting, at times hopelessly frustrating and, above all, unforgettable. Peggy was 64 when she died and while, to some, that age may falsely imply she had lived a full life – there was still a limitless amount of mischievousness and vitality within her when destiny shortened her journey.

I was in my early thirties when we lost Peggy. Hers was a life traumatized by calamity, rooted in early loss – packaged in laughter.

She married the love of her life at 17, only to lose him to an inherited blood disorder months after she brought their only child, a son, into the world. Widowed at 22, she would raise her son with the help of her devoted parents, my Uncle Jimmy and Aunt Margaret, and live to celebrate her son's wedding, the birth of his daughter, and the ups and downs of a life surrounded by friends and family in the South Philadelphia neighborhood, just four city blocks away from Mifflin Street, that was her lifetime home.

Peggy was my father's first cousin (Uncle Jimmy and Grandpop Tony where brothers) in fact, his older cousin, but to me she was *more* than a cousin, not *exactly* like a big sister, not quite an aunt, not really a best friend, far from a role model ... more like a kindred *spirit*.

No matter how old I was, the little girl in her, no matter how old she was, knew how to talk to the little girl in me – to cut through the years, the circumstances, and connect with joy, even in heartache. I always felt like she was on my level, and the older I got, the older she got to match me. Still, somehow, as my youth turned into adulthood, it was Peggy, not me, who retained a glimmer of innocence, an appreciation for discovery and a hope in miracles.

She was unfeigned and spontaneous, trusting, and immature.

Peggy was humor in despair.

She was laughter in sadness.

She was a child of wonder, until the day she died at age 64.

It was Peggy who taught me how to play a practical joke. One of my favorites, going to the second floor of the Mifflin Street house with a bowl filled with water, and strategically sprinkling the water out an open bedroom window, right down on the heads of Grandpop Tony and whoever else was gathered outside the house, talking, or smoking, while sitting atop the steps. It was Peggy who replaced coffee creamer with chocolate milk. It was Peggy who loosened the tops of the saltshakers. It was Peggy who would hide in the closet and stay there as long as it took for you to find her – then jump scare you! It was Peggy who found the funny in the boring. It was Peggy who would, when I faced my own obstacles in young adulthood, bring a surprising moment of seriousness to our times together, cautioning me to make better decisions in my life, than she had in her life. She could be serious, she probably was always serious in her heart, but what she showed the world was what she dreamed to be: Carefree, and complete.

I always wondered how she survived after the loss of her husband, so young.

The laughter in the trees inched closer to me. Peggy's youthful beauty put me at ease, and as I looked at her, I started laughing too, warm tears rolled down my cheeks as Peggy moved closer to me, reaching out her hands for me to take them, which I did. Her hands were warm, her smile widened, as she looked at me, I could see Peggy's spontaneous nature was very much still devilishly and brilliantly alive.

"Hey Pen, how are you sweetheart," Peggy said to me, drifting our hands back and forth as if we were carrying something together. As my arms swayed, moved by her own, I could feel the years peel away from me, leaving me feeling lighter, and somehow, happier. I felt as if I had no problems in my life, no bills, no illness, no stresses, no loss, and no fear. My hair was again longer, curls and waves of brilliant brownish auburn rolling over my shoulders, bobbing and lifting with every sway of my arms still in motion with Peggy's weightless ethereality.

"Peggy, what a surprise, it's good to see you, you look amazing," I told my older cousin, who, in this moment, looked decades younger than my age. Looking into her blue eyes I could see her effervescence, her blood and bone exuberance, her animated cheeriness, not dimmed in the more than 25 years since she breathed air. She still radiated fun – and a hint of trouble.

"Peggy, I, I cannot, I mean, I can't believe this, you are so young, you look beautiful," my tears rolling as I spoke to her. "There is no one like you. We all still really miss you. Oh, your son and his family, everyone is doing great, all are well, your granddaughter has a beautiful daughter of her own now, everyone is happy and safe and well – and so much of you is still in so much of all of them, even your little granddaughter, she has your sparkling eyes."

"Oh, I know," Peggy said to me, her smile boosting in sunniness, as she rested our swinging arms and, with a squeeze, released mine. "That baby is so pretty, isn't she? She's beautiful."

Peggy's great granddaughter was beautiful, filled with adventure and wonder. How could she not be, with Peggy's spirit watching over her.

"Yes, definitely. She's adorable, and so much fun, and so smart," I said to Peggy. "I see you in her too, Peggy, that little look in her eye, especially when she's being silly, or when she's mad," I laughed. "She's full of energy and fun, just like you – she's going to be a powerful woman."

Peggy smiled at me.

"You're a powerful woman yourself," she said.

Calming her face, she took on a serene expression. "You know, I never wanted you to be like me, not like me," she told me. "I didn't want you to face any disappointments, not like the ones I faced, not like the loss that hit me. I wanted you to have it all."

Together, we began to walk down the trail, the dirt and gravel, somehow, crunching only under my feet.

"Do you remember me telling you that I didn't want you to end up like me?" Peggy asked. "It was after you had your daughter, your husband was so sick, and you had so much going on. The bills. The doctors. The not knowing if your husband would even make it. All I could think of was your life was going to be like mine. I didn't want you to have a harder life."

I knew Peggy saw that similarity in us – I realized it years ago.

My husband was diagnosed with Type I diabetes the same month we found out I was pregnant with our first daughter. He was an extremely brittle diabetic, resulting in ambulance calls, hospital stays and one brief coma in the months it took me to carry our first baby girl to her birth. As I gained 60 pounds, he lost that and more, his body succumbing to the ravages of blood sugars out of control, despite medical intervention and his own efforts to control his out-of-control body. Fortunately, as the years went on, he was able to adjust and, with the help of insulin pumps, keep his blood sugars controlled enough to end the regular hospital emergencies. He was able to build his body back, almost. He was able to raise his children.

"I didn't want you to struggle, to have sickness and everything that comes with it hit you so early, so young,"

Peggy said as we walked, her strawberry chiffon gown flowing in the summer breeze, swishing and swooshing in the air like pink mist. "You know what happened to me."

I took her hand as we walked.

"I know, Peggy, you had it so hard. For me, for my life, things improved. My husband was able to raise our kids and be a really great Dad," I told her. "It was hard, at times, I think everyone has it hard really, I don't know anyone without struggle and sacrifice, but we made it, we raised our kids, and they are really great people," I told her, giving her warm hand a gentle squeeze. "It was a good life."

Peggy stopped walking.

"It still is a good life, Penny," Peggy said to me, taking my open hand in her open hand, so that we were facing one another, gripping each other in a lock that felt like a knowing embrace of sisterhood. Two women who, when emerging into their married lives, realized their partners would have chronic, extremely dangerous health issues. For Peggy, those health issues were catastrophic, leaving her to be both father and mother to her son – when she was barely grown herself.

"You know, as hard as things were for me, as tough as it was at times, losing my husband so early, worrying about every decision I made my whole life, things were hard for me, maybe too hard, but I always wanted more. I never for one minute wanted less. Not less struggle. Not less decisions. Not less time. I always wanted more," Peggy shared. "You need to want more too."

Why were my tears flowing so much with Peggy?

"I know, I know," I told her. "The past few years, for me, have been challenging, tougher than life has been in a long time, but I am beginning to feel better, more hopeful," I told her. "I'm beginning, especially after everything today, everything right now, to want more – to see that my life can have more and be more – that I have more to do, and more laughter to create."

Peggy smiled, hugged me and, turning me toward the path again, we regained our steps.

I could, again, only hear my feet crushing over the gravel.

Peggy seemed to float.

I wondered if she was floating, I couldn't see her feet under her gown.

As I continued walking, submerged in moments with Peggy, we talked about her mother, and the funny stories of how her mother and my Grandmom Philly would argue over nothing, then forget it all when it was time for a bridal shower or holiday. We joked about her dog Prince, who never liked anyone except her.

We shared tears over her father, remembering stories of his stoic nature, and generous heart. We talked about her son. We talked about my kids. We reminisced about Mifflin Street. We shared our favorite water ice flavors. I filled her in on my Dad's health issues. She said she already knew.

I filled Peggy in on my Mom.

She said she already knew.

Our conversation was filled with words, and at the same time, there were moments I couldn't tell if we were actually speaking to one another or experiencing the same thoughts.

Then, Peggy slowed down.

I slowed my pace to match hers, until she stopped entirely.

"I'm so glad you are so strong," Peggy said to me. "When you want to cry, cry. When you want to laugh, laugh. When you want to feel, feel. Don't ever, don't never, never, ever, let life take that away from you, no matter what life does to you, don't ever let life take away the moments when you want to laugh, to cry, to feel."

"I won't, Peggy, I promise." I assured her.

Peggy smiled and took a few steps back.

She didn't speak to me, but her expression told me all I needed to know in this moment. As she took a few more paces back, the gravel under her began to glow, a brilliant sunshine gold that encircled her elegant frame, and illuminated the flush rose tones of her gown.

A robust breeze began to blow her red hair around her face, her thick waves pushing around her ample cheeks and brilliant smile. She was aglow with a radiance, as if Peggy, herself, was light. As I watched her, realizing this was her exit from my journey, sunbeams seemed to flow from her fingers to the ground.

As I watched her shine, she began to disappear before my eyes, joining the sunbeams that she seemed to create, as she drifted into the glow that surrounded her, smiling at me as she lost her form, unfolding with pageantry and splendor as the final whirl of her gown kissed the air.

I heard her voice.

Keep going, Penny.

Remember to laugh.

Alone With Everyone

As I continued alone, I felt at ease. No longer pensive. No longer curious or impatient to see what was ahead. I felt restored emotionally, but a bit exhausted physically. I wanted to stop walking and allow myself to feel the flood of love, sympathy, concern, and affection that seemed to fill the air. I wanted to process everything, to absorb this surreal experience.

The dirt trail narrowed to a thin passage just the right size for one person to navigate. I thought I heard my Uncle Mike calling my name. Once again, the hint of warm, baked apples filled the air. The faint ting, ting, tingling of Sammie's collar echoed in the distance. I thought I heard my mother and father's voices, too, talking about what's for dinner. In the dirt, as I moved forward, I could see the prominent indent of a perfect circle, just like Aunt Elvira's metal bucket. A thick, cool breeze broke the warmth of the moment, with hints of sweet cinnamon and apples riding the breeze. I took a few more steps and I noticed, looking down, an old, worn hammer in the dirt. A sign of a Cedar Avenue revisit, perhaps, or a clue to my next familial encounter.

Looking down again, in the dirt, a coin glistened in the sun.

A penny.

I never preferred to be alone, but, at the same time, I was fine with just my company. Walking the woods with no other signs of people, only the blurring sights, light flickering hints and audible detection that I was not alone. I was not walking alone at all. I was walking, in a way, with everyone – everyone and anyone along on this journey that I did not, could not, foresee.

"Alone is … relative," I said out loud, to no one … to everyone. Feeling certain I was not alone at all; I spoke to the air.

"Hey … *Everyone*, thank you for being here, I appreciate you all, and I know you are here for me today. I feel you." I spoke softly out to the trees and bushes, to the bugs and squirrels and chipmunks, to the bees and sunbeams. To the family members lingering all around me, beyond my ability to see, disembodied voices of assurance, and comfort.

More voices.

More laughter.

More conversations humming over the treetops.

The sound of hammering drifting over the trail.

Tones of big band music animating the air.

Flashes of light, golden confetti sparkles, glittering beams of light popping from trees to ground. Distant tones of music. The tingling of Sammie's collar. Clanking glasses. As I walked slowly forward, I could see silhouettes in the shadows, women, men, children. Some dancing. Some running. Some waving. On both sides of me, filling the trail edges and deep into the thick of abundant tree trunks, lush greenery and the enthralling prominence of New England rocks and boulders.

At one turn of the trail, I saw my beautiful, vivacious cousin Michelle, who died way too young, at just 40.

Michelle was dancing into a radiant sunbeam that was magnificently poised between two huge trees, as if the beam of light was waiting to catch her. Smiling my way, with hands over her head as she twirled with abandon, Michelle looked healthy and strong. No longer shackled to the obstructive forces that impeded her life. She was liberated, beautifully liberated of the addictive leanings that brought her life to an all-too-soon conclusion. Electrifyingly captivating, her raven hair gloriously flowed around her head and shoulders. She stopped twirling and skipping long enough to look directly at me, smile widely and put her right hand up, offering a subtle wave that generated a calmness. Putting her right hand back down to her side, Michelle lifted her eyebrows and gestured for me to keep going down the trail, before she smiled large again and, with a few quick steps, disappeared into a sunbeam that was so thick in composition she appears more to be diving into a gelatinous formation of molten lava.

In stepping forward, looking to my left and right, I felt an amplified warmth on my shoulders.

Cousins, aunts, uncles, friends. A parade of names marching through my mind. A vision of faces in figment s of light and haze. Voices, hushed in conversation, some in laughter and praise. The people. The everyone.

Too many entities, so many names, flooding my mind – filling the space around me.

My first cousin Jennie, still very much alive and well in the *'real'* world I had been a part of only this morning, now, somehow, appearing as a little girl running barefoot in the grass straight into a shower of thinly glittering beams of sunlight.

We would spend summers together, Jennie and I, swimming in her pool, fighting over Barbie adventures, laughing at nothing and everything, and telling ghost stories late at night. In the *real* world, wherever, whenever that may be in this moment, Jennie is a busy mother of two very grown sons and the owner of a wildly successful online marketing agency. She's two years older than I am actually, in the *real* world. Right now, though, she's a little girl, running barefoot in the dirt, clutching a Barbie as she hops over fallen tree trunks, skipping toward sunbeams that seem to play with her, dancing around her as she hops over them. The little girl, *little Jennie*, gave me a big wave as she continued chasing the beams of sun. I could see her little feet, blackened on their bottoms from playing in the dirt, as she ran through the grass and twigs, skipping joyfully and singing to the wind.

I'll have to remember to tell Jennie all about this experience. Jennie may be the only person who might believe me.

My best friends from first grade, Judith and Diana, looking no more than age 6 or 7. The sounds of a baseball game in the distance. My father's voice telling one of his legendary funny stories about Grandpop Tony. I think this one is the time he cheated at poker. Our neighbor, Nicole, laughing and smiling with her younger siblings, Shannon, and Don, like family to us when I was growing up in the two-story home that my parents always made feel safe, like a kingdom they lovingly lorded over, a bountiful haven for any and all. My Aunt Jean, or Miss Jean, as I lovingly knew her, sitting on a boulder. My good friend Carrie, a sister in spirit, playing her purple guitar against a tree. A collection of some of my greatest soul connections in life, friends and soul pieces, Jeanine, Maryann, Rose, Sandy, Suzy.

Everyone was everywhere.

Some who had lived before I was even born. Many still alive and well right now, but in another place in time, in another part of their own lives, perhaps even on their own walks. I felt included in this great assembly of energy, of persons – past, present, maybe even future – amassed to bring me encouragement. I was part of a congregation, one of eternal reach and imperishable limits.

A congregation immemorial.

*A kingdom of **my very own.***

I could see the markings of footprints of all sizes in the dirt now, some appearing alongside and near me as I continued down the trail. There was one set of footprints that appeared larger, and a yard or so ahead of me, pushing into the dirt before me, but stopping if I slowed to wait for me. I felt an overwhelming sense of acceptance and love coming at me from everywhere.

I was truly walking alone, with ***everyone***.

It was as if everyone got an invitation to a party in my honor. I felt like the luckiest girl in the world. As soon as I had this thought, I was treated to the gift of seeing two of my favorite people. Stepping slowly forward, deciding to savor this experience, and with the soft tones of ting, ting, ting that told me my beloved dog was still very nearby, I saw Joe and Mary Jo.

When you are part of a big family, you are a drop in an ocean. Two of the greatest waves in the ocean of my father's family were Joe and Mary Jo.

Joe was my father's older cousin on his father's side. A direct line from Grandpop Tony's tapestry, Joe, the oldest son of Grandpop Tony's oldest sister, and Mary Jo, his loving wife of more than 50 years, were favorites of the family, producing two sons, four daughters, and, at the time of their deaths more than 25 years ago, 14 grandchildren which, over the passing of years, grew to a higher number resulting in great grandchildren nearing 18 as of this moment in time.

The line of people created by their love would stretch from New Jersey to California. A mighty community of people, from two lovebirds who never had quite enough money to ease life's burdens, but, with their six children, never wanted for a single thing. They comforted me when Grandmom Philly died. Seeing them at her funeral played over and over in my mind as the years became decades. Joe actually made me laugh that day. I can still see them, in that moment, inches from Grandmom Philly's dead body, displayed for her viewing, Joe and Mary Jo, leaned into me and each gave such comfort, it broke me from the darkness of my sorrow for a few minutes and brought me back into the light.

I would always remember them in that moment, which, sadly, would be the last moment I would have in Joe's company and, as life would dictate, one of the last in Mary Jo's as well.

Joe passed away just two weeks after Grandmom Philly, suddenly while on a trip with Mary Jo. Mary Jo, always the strength of her family, and all who knew her, would live on a few more months before the Good Lord called her to be with her Joe. Their family, six children, a community of grandchildren, the very beginnings of great grandchildren, would carry on their love.

Yet here they were again…helping to bring me into the light. Cheering me up, with the radiance of their love for one another, and our shared family connection.

Joe and Mary Jo waved at me, well, she with her right hand up and waving, and Joe with his arms around her thin waist, both nodding and smiling in my direction. If there were ever two people who completed one another – it was Joe and Mary Jo. My Grandpop Tony adored his nephew Joe, he adored Mary Jo even more, and would spend weekends, and sometimes weeks, visiting at their home in Somerdale, New Jersey, playing cards with Joe until late into the night and, in the days, fixing anything Mary Jo needed tending to around the house – clogged sink, a dryer that refused to spin wet laundry, smashed window pane, whatever broken down car was in the driveway that particular year. Nothing was out of reach of Grandpop Tony's homespun repairs.

As I waved at both, I could not hold back the warm tears slowly washing my eyes – the sight of them together, it was magic. Smiling together, they turned away a bit, but not before Joe called out to me *"Keep going, Penny, keep going, going, going. Enjoy yourself, you're doing great. Better than I did when I had this happen to me, I'll tell you that. Keep going, kid."* With Mary Jo nodding in agreement, they looked up to the tree canopy as if their next steps would take them straight up through the leaves that swayed over their heads. Joe's hands around Mary Jo's waist were unflinching. Even in the afterlife, or the forever life, or whatever this life right now may be, these two people were one.

My eyes, wet with tears, caused me to blink a few times, and briefly look down. Almost immediately I brought my head back up to gaze again in their direction.

They were gone.

The tree limbs above where they had stood were moving wildly and, in the air, there lingered what looked like thousands of miniature fireworks popping, dazzling sparks and brilliant flashes everywhere Joe and Mary Jo had been, leaving the air almost electric, bursting with the love that overflowed from them. I felt the hair on my arms stand up a bit. I looked around, in all directions, but Joe and Mary Jo were nowhere. Only flickers and flares of gold in the sunbeams. No trace of them, just the spectacle of the hauntingly miraculous flashes they left behind.

I wondered if they had always been magic.

The Rain Monster

The sky began to look gloomy as I kept my pace forward. The clouds were changing from calming and white, growing in quantity above me and especially off in the distance, hovering above the path's treetops, now dulling swirls and colossal lumps of blackish gray, almost completely shrouding the lingering hint of copper from the still present sun. The clouds were enormous, wrinkled in thick layers with flat bottoms that seemed to be painted by the sky itself, turning the landscape bleak.

So many shadows, born from the stillness of the cloud cover, finding home in dissipating veils of light. The air felt like something was coming, that feeling when the weather almost turns to menacing, as the sky changes personalities with a threatening intimidation.

I remembered a story my father told me, when he was a boy, growing up on Mifflin Street.

One day as he played on the corner, a storm thundered down the street toward him. He saw it move, from blocks and blocks away, through the lines and edges of the cement corners that framed his village of South Philly, over the bricks and mortar of the neighborhoods that raised him, and his mother, and his father, a torrential monster drenching rooftops, cars and streets, inch upon inch, until he watched it literally stop over the middle of Mifflin Street, just out of reach of where he stood. There the storm hovered, dark and powerful, it drowned half of Mifflin Street in so much rain that people who were outside ran for their front doors, doused with rain soaking through their clothing before they even realized how inundated in water, how very permeated, they already were as the storm swilled and churned above.

My father, just a boy, was in awe of this spectacle, seeing the storm as a creature, just out of reach of him, as if it spared him its deluge on purpose. It was his encounter with a rain monster, his boyish bravery keeping him locked in its gaze.

As I walked forward, the storm clouds now right above my head, and I beneath their increasing potency, I noticed the earthy path, etched by bushes and branches, seemed to crisp up its edges, as if the shadows were linear, bouncing bits of light off of shapes that replicated the angles of brick walls and front doors. These invisible structures, on either side of me, were illuminated by the glistening drips of rain that now fell from the sky onto me. I noticed raindrops flowing down invisible walls and what appeared to be frames of doors.

As I walked down the now moistened path, with tiny pockets and wells of dirt more aqueous than comfortable for my tired sneakers, I realized I was walking down a translucent version of Mifflin Street, a soppy, misty echo, dripping from the storm above, cushioning me from the brunt of the showery pour and escalating winds.

A crack of thunder detonated, bursting like a cannon fired in the distance. The ground shook, as a peeling discharge of rain rumbled toward me, a torrent of water, a frightening bank of rain moving, like a monster, down the path in my direction.

Until it stopped.

As if restricted from proceeding over me, I watched it shudder and shift, drenching the invisible corners and edges of the intangible Mifflin Street that stood on either side of me, like a protector. The rain was terrifyingly strong, and beautiful at the same time, a force of supernatural nature tempered, barred from flowing over me, leaving me to watch its display. I saw it move over Mifflin Street, just in sight of me, and yet, unable to take me in its power. My father must have felt that way as a boy, watching his rain monster overtake the Mifflin Street that protected him.

Was this the same storm, the same rain monster, that my father saw as a boy? If it was, I can see why he remembered it.

"Hey, what are you waiting for over there," a young voice called out to me.

It was a boy.

Was it my *father?*

The young voice seemed to control the weather, and, within a few seconds of hearing the boy call out, from exactly here I was not sure, the restrained storm diminished entirely, reducing in velocity until it evaporated into the invisible Mifflin Street that refused to prescribe to it.

"Hey, how are you over there?"

The boy called out again, this time it sounded like he was nearer to me.

As the sun began to poke through the spreading clouds, the figment of the boy came into focus. He was dressed in old-fashioned clothing and looked just like the picture I grew up seeing in my Grandmom Philly's bedroom. Her older brother, Louis.

Why was he here?

Then again, why wouldn't he be here?

I thought about how short his life was, how unfair it was for him to be so stricken, so young. I thought about how my Grandmom Philly would talk about her brother, and, throughout her lifetime, wondered what he might have been had he been gifted the opportunity to grow up.

"Louis, is that you?" I called out to the boy, who by this point was walking straight at me. "I'm Penny, your sister's Philly's granddaughter."

"I know who you are," the boy said to me, a little sheepish, but surprisingly resolute, as he stopped directly in front of me. He looked me up and down, then reached his hand out for me to take hold. I reached out, grabbed his small hand, and looked at his angelic face.

His was really the face of an angel.

"You are doing good today, Penny," my great uncle told me. Squeezing my hand, a bit, he started walking, me in tow, and a few paces ahead he stopped. He reached my hand up to his mouth and gave it a little kiss. Letting go of my hand, he pointed forward.

"You are almost done," Louis told me. "We're all … so proud of you."

His words were so sweetly delivered. What a wonderful little boy Louis must have been, so brave in his sickness. What a heartbreak for my Grandmom Philly's mother, to lose her only son.

"Thank you, Uncle Louis," I said to the boy. He was a boy, but also an eternal being – innocent and wise, young, and very, very old. I thought about the stories my Grandmom Philly would tell me of him, how hard it was when he died, how they laid his little body out in a wooden casket for family and friends to pay their respects as Louis drifted from boy to memory. His little casket sat in the living room of the Mifflin Street house for two days.

"You're going to walk around that turn, and when you see him, you'll stop," Louis told me. "You are doing really good today, Penny, and … *happy birthday my dearest.*"

"Thank you, Uncle Louis," I told the small boy, smiling at the delightful boy who was born the second year of the First World War. Looking into his face, his brown eyes, the shape of his cheeks and jawline, the waves of his hair over his eyes, he looked so much like my Grandmom Philly.

"You are remarkable, Uncle Louis." I told the haunting boy who died more than 50 years before my birth.

"I think … I think, you know, we are all remarkable," he said, and, with that, the little boy who was my great uncle gestured for me to continue down the trail.

Louis took a few paces back once I started moving forward and, turning my head to see him off, I caught him running at full pace down the trail until he disappeared into a million sparkles of yellow and gold. Under his racing feet, the still muddy dirt shot off bursts of what looked like tiny sparklers, popping like miniature bottle rockets, illuminating the soil particles as he rushed over them. It was as if the ground was electrified, short circuiting as Uncle Louis bolted over it, perhaps rushing back to his version of Mifflin Street, where his remarkable people lived.

I wondered if my father, as a boy, waited for Uncle Louis somewhere on Mifflin Street, so that the two of them could combine their courage to face rain monsters together.

Celebrated

As I continued down the trail, my backpack over my shoulder, I began to wonder if this was all happening in one day, or if I was in a place that contained no measurement of time at all. My mind was filled with thoughts. I felt invigorated, not physically, but emotionally. I felt enlivened and ready to uplift my attitude and intentions. I felt like a person of faith, a person renewed, and realigned.

I was still me, but maybe more me than I had been in years. Once again, lost in my thoughts, it took a few moments for me to be aware of them all.

A was walking with everyone … *again.*

My father-in-law, Omar, who died when my kids were still little. I saw my Uncle Mikey and Aunt Marie again, sitting at a table playing cards with Grandmom Philly and Grandpop Tony. There was little Michael, running through the bushes. Aunt Elvira was talking to her nieces Loretta and Rosemarie, with their husbands nearby, Dick and Max. Some were flashes of faces in the trees, others were fully engaged in whatever they were doing, stopping to smile my way, wave me forward or even offer some words of encouragement for my journey.

My mother's Granny. My cousin Terry, all the way from Iowa – if that's where this version of him resides. Some were dancing, others walking through the density of the bushes, keeping to the sunbeams that poked holes in the tree canopy.

When I turned my head I noticed Pop Pop in the distance, scouting for a fine tree to cut down to build his next project. A little girl running around him, her tomboy strides and toothless grin the reflection of my mother when she was a girl. There were old women knitting by a boulder, sitting together with yarn everywhere as they each created blankets and sweaters from the tips of their knitting needles and wooden hooks. I recognized these women from faded, old pictures stored in boxes. It was my Grandmom Philly's grandmother, and her sisters.

I saw my own father, looking no more than 30, carrying a huge sporting bag flung over his shoulder, burgeoning with basketballs, walking swiftly as if heading off to a game and looking every bit the dedicated coach he had been for over 50 years, championing three generations of elementary school basketball players. Walking behind my father was my younger brother, Joey, in his boyhood form, working hard to keep strides with our force of nature Dad.

I saw my first-grade teacher, Sister Theresa, one of the many Sisters of Mercy from Trim, Ireland, to teach at the Catholic elementary school my brother and I attended. I saw two of my Grandmom Philly's favorite cousins, Rose and Anthony, both gone from this world for many decades. Yet, here they stood, alive and well, sitting at a small table, sipping coffee, smiling at me.

Almost knocking me over, my childhood friend, Kathy Voorhees, riding her bike over the gravel and dirt. Her little legs pounding the pedals of her red bicycle, she tapped my side as she whooshed past me, yelling for me to get my bike and join her. I'm not sure if the wheels of her bike touched the ground.

Every face, familiar.

Every face, a memory.

Every face, a miracle.

My eyes taking me from one face to the next, one soul to the next, with generations of family, mixing with a lifetime of friends, colleagues, neighbors, lovers, all glimpses of parts of my life and my experiences, all etching together to form a living portrait that meticulously painted itself before my eyes. I couldn't predict who I would see, or why I would see them, whether they would speak to me, or simply show themselves as part of my surreal new reality. All were a blessing to see though, as all took me to a point in time when I reconnected with my own soul.

All joining me for the walk of my lifetime.

As I moved further down the dirt trail, I noticed, up ahead, in the clearing, a glorious opening of the sun-drenched trees and bushes. As I made my way to the clearing, I noticed golden flakes were suddenly adorning the dirt trail, golden rose pedals, as if sprinkled by a flower girl in an elaborate bridal procession. As I stepped toward over the increasing number of golden pedals, further down the trail, the path opened to a breathtaking blue sky. The density of the bushes and trees carved a line out of the trail, forming a gateway between it and the increasingly expansive clearing ahead, all under the ownership of the supernaturally vivid azure sky.

It was there that I saw her. Off in the distance, sitting on a small hill, my Mom Mom. Born in London before Queen Elizabeth II was a glimmer in her mother's eye, Julia was her *name* before Mom Mom became her *title*. She would lose both of her parents when she was very young, first her father, then her mother, leaving herself and six siblings to finish raising one another in the town of Chester, very near her future home of Upland. It was there the family settled after sailing from London to New York when she was just a girl. She would grow from girl to woman in Chester. In Upland, she would grow from Julia to Mom Mom over decades of raising children, baking Depression cakes, and traveling the ups and downs of life with her love, the man who grew from Francis Xavier to Pop Pop.

There she was, though, in this moment, looking very much like only Julia.

Mom Mom was young, wearing an incandescent violet dress. Appearing no more than 18 or so, she waved softly at me as she seemed to hover inches above the ground, with sparks of gold glimmering around her and sunbeams soaking into her ebony hair. She glowed with a healthy vitality, the promise of youth, as Julia, which would fade as time would transition her from Julia to Mom Mom. This young version of Mom Mom was snappy, with a venturesomeness that zested from her. A young woman, filled with sparkle and stamina, ready to bring her fervor to the world. I had never seen Mom Mom display such charisma in the time I knew her.

Of course, to be fair, who of us retains the glorious glow of youth forever?

By the time I was born, Mom Mom had suffered several strokes, leaving her weak and incapable of communicating without the struggle of pushing out her words, which, despite her best efforts, were garbled and mumbled utterings, supported by mild hand motions. Sometimes, that effort to try to talk was too much for her, she would do simple gestures, like a little wave, or a gentle hand hold, or even put her thumb to her nose and wiggle her fingers at me with the silliness of a teenager. Due to her health issues, she would never be able to cradle me, never be able to hold me without my mother supporting my tiny baby body. Mom Mom would never be able to bake me a cake or show me how she made Pop Pop's favorite cookies. She couldn't tell me long and detailed stories of what my mother was like as a little girl.

She couldn't tell me any of her stories at all.

My mother, her youngest baby, would take my brother and I to visit Mom Mom and Pop Pop at least one Sunday each month at their Cedar Avenue home. Mom Mom would almost always be in her bed, upstairs, watching a movie. As I walked up the stairs to visit with her, I would find her, tiny and frail, laying on her right side and facing the television. Mom Mom's soft curls beautifully framed her divinely wrinkled face, giving a hint to the beauty she was in her youth.

The beauty looking at me right now.

Looking straight at her, as she beamed at me, I saw only a fresh and earnest young woman of strength, capable of anything as she glowed with a luminousness that soberly extinguished my memories of the pale old woman I knew all those years ago, ravaged by illness, but somehow always managing to hint, with her sweet bluish green eyes, that, once upon a time, she was nothing short of entrancing. As I walked almost to the point that I could see the color of her lipstick, she began to fade into the air, her beauty diffused by the buzzing of golden streams that purposefully, almost intently, adorned her small frame.

Before her girlish face drifted into the air, she smiled at me, raised her thumb to her nose and wiggled her free fingers playfully.

I laughed.

She laughed.

And then, she was gone.

As I continued my walk, I lost count of the people I saw, the faces, the friends, the family, all splendidly enveloped in swirling, glittering, golden beams of light. Everyone looked blessed, almost saintly, glorified by a golden hue so jubilant I was certain the ground on which each showed themselves to me must be sacred. It was as if the remote Maine trail transformed into the aisle of a grand and imposing church, and every person I encountered was a parishioner , all ordained in a kind of timelessness. All blessed in a shared, magical experience.

My magical experience.

I felt celebrated, sanctified, even extraordinary. Imaginary or not, with each step I took on my walk alone, my walk with *everyone*, I felt more spiritual, more fulfilled in my soul, than I had my entire adult life. I felt greater than myself, more spectral, less mortal, as if every step carried me to immortality.

My Mother

It must have been at least an hour after I saw my Mom Mom, that the trail stretched me forward. In some places, the trail grew wide, other spots the trail was a mere inch, with leaves and tiny limbs hugging me as I stepped forward. At one point, the trail seemed to stop altogether, my feet encountering overgrown grass. I looked around. Trees everywhere, even behind me.

Where was the trail?

I found myself wondering:

What would my mother do?

She would drift forward, of course, and, with that, I took tiny drags forward with my feet, pushing the fresh soil, inch by inch, until, as if being opened by my insistence it must exist, the trail welcomed me again, first only a few inches wide, then more, and a little more, until it was many feet across and unmistakably ready for me. My mother was not one to give up when faced with obstacles. She was always one to find a way, figure it out, make the right move.

The breeze seemed to pick up as I hastened my steps on the now very wide trail.

I was in my late twenties when the prospect of my parents dying became a very real part of my life. Of course, I always knew how fortunate I was to have young parents. My mother lost both of her parents before she was 35. My father lost his father in his early thirties. Grandmom Philly lived long enough to see my Dad enter his fifties and, mercifully, died just months before my father faced the first real threat to his own mortality. Cancer. My Dad would go on to battle his way through two cancer traumas and a major cardiac procedure. My Mom, starting her medical challenges in her early 60s, would herself endure multiple strokes and declining renal function.

Still, into their 70s, they endured.

They dreamed.

They planned. They fought. They loved. They laughed.

The boy from South Philly with the roaring personality.

The shy girl from Upland.

As I walked forward on the trail, tiring from the day, I found myself thinking of my parents, my father, back home in New Jersey, and my mother, somewhere in the eternal sparkles of life after life, somewhere hopefully with her mother by her side, my Mom Mom, maybe they were both right now, somewhere hopefully watching over me, somewhere maybe on this trail with me in this very moment.

I saw my grandparents. I had seen family and friends, ancestors young and old. I had seen friends and family who are still of this world, yet in different ages and times, renditions of loved ones showing themselves in different forms, perhaps echoing through time. I had not yet seen my husband, in any form, young or older, as a flash of a shadow, or speaking to me. And, I had not seen my mother. I wondered if they would make appearances, or, perhaps, if I could wish them to do so. If I thought about them hard enough, reverberated on what was left of the energy they each gave me in life, could I make them join me on this journey.

Are they here?

Where is my mother?

My mother died when she was 75 on All Saints Day, wrapped in my arms, devoid of color in her beautiful cheeks, as she took her final labored breaths from this life before moving willingly to her next adventure. Every year on November 1, many Roman Catholics and other Christians around the world observe All Saints Day, which honors all saints of the church deemed to have attained heaven.

All Saints Day was a fitting day for her to leave us. She was, in all ways, the saint of our family, the very best of us – our gold. The years and months leading up to my mother's death were a journey we shared. The doctor appointments. The hospital stays. The rehabilitation facilities collected during her final years, four different facilities following various hospital runs. My mother left me slowly, then very quickly. Bits and pieces of her, tiny little shattered fragments of her vitality and function, with each stroke, with each low blood pressure episode, with each ticking moment closer to total renal failure, with all of these declining realities my beautiful mother was leaving me, leaving all of us, but slowly.

Until, with her final hospital stay, the slow quickened to rapid, and then, to nothing.

My mother's final days I rarely left her side, sleeping with her in her hospital room, making her goodbye calls with her to select childhood friends, and treasured friends and family throughout her lifetime. I held her for hours. We sang hymns. We watched movies. We sipped ice-cold Cokes. We held hands for hours at a time, until one or both of us fell asleep in the grip of the other. We greeted her sisters, her nieces and, of course, she spent treasured moments with my father and brother, her only son, the little boy who chased dinosaurs with her leading his way.

I would tell her, in those final days, final hours, I didn't know how to do anything without her. What would I do without her? How would I do anything without her? Teaching me how to be a loving mother until the very end, she selflessly told me, in response to my questions of how I could ever go forward without her: You're already doing it.

You're already doing it…

I was already doing it?

Shortly after those words, the shy girl from Upland was ready to let go.

When my mother died, a part of me felt somehow less alive, but mostly, and in ways I cannot explain, I felt strong, buffered by her strength and the quiet coaching she gave me in her final days. I could be resilient. I would be strong. I was ready to let her go. In the most remarkable and unremarkable of moments, as much a quiet catastrophe as the gifting of eternal life, my mother let herself drift away from me, knowing she had left me with all she could, and it would be up to me to use it to the best of my abilities. To the best of who I was and who I could still grow to be.

I don't think anyone ever really gets over the loss of their mother.

Before my mother belonged to all of us, though, before she belonged to me, and I to her, she was a girl who loved the ocean. My mother was 15 when my father, just 18, spotted her and a friend walking on the boardwalk of Atlantic City, New Jersey, on a sun-soaked July afternoon. My Mom and her best friend were chaperoned by my grandmother who, fortunately for my Mom and her friend, gave the girls lots of freedom. That summer stay in Atlantic City was a fun one for my Mom, and also a life changer.

She met her future husband.

And she almost died.

The summer vacation was predictable enough. My Mom and her friend, Gerry Pierce, woke up early each day, enjoyed big breakfasts presented by my grandmother, morning after morning, then the girls rushed out to spend hours on the beach.

One day they swam out into the ocean.

And swam.

And swam.

And swam.

And swam.

Too far. My Mom and Gerry were out, way beyond where their toes could hope to scrape the sandy bottom of the shoreline. Out beyond the rolling waves that break at your hips and thighs, the ones you see coming, the ones you jump over, as you stand on the beach, wading in the shallows, safe from the depths, while mindful that undertows and rip currents are lurking. Safely planted, feet sinking into the wet sand, anyone who has spent time enjoying a day at the beach knows the cool thrill of the crashing, little waves that enthusiastically push and pull the ocean to the beach, announcing its arrival with a playful, watery smash.

The girls were nowhere near safely planted.

In fact, my Mom and her friend were not safe at all.

Swimming and bobbing in the waves, out just about where the ocean could take them, they realized their exuberance outperformed their practicality. They looked at each other, eyes in an almost panic, realizing it was only the push of their arms and kicking of their legs that kept their chins above the waterline. They could see families sprawled out on the beach, with colorful umbrellas crafting rainbow swirls just beyond the breaking waves that pushed to shore. If one girl had panicked, the day could have ended in disaster, as neither girl was an exceptional swimmer. Instead, without a hint of panic, only an acceptance of their situation, the girls began to motion their shoulders toward the beach, allowing their legs to kick behind them as they patiently drifted on the rolling waves.

One wave after the next, one little bump of water after the next, the girls bobbed and floated their way stoically to where they could, at last, plant their feet on the shoreline once again. My mother and her friend made a great team, in that moment of silent acceptance. Together, they drifted and drifted, and calmly willed themselves to safety.

This was a story my mother would tell me on many occasions, partly because it was just a great story, and mostly because it carried with it a lesson in staying calm in adversity, of finding a resolve in a crisis and, above all else, of moving forward – even if you had to drift.

I felt I was drifting right now. Drifting forward toward I knew not what, with a slight breeze on my shoulders. One foot after the other, drifting slowly down this unearthly wooded trail.

My mind filled of thoughts of my Mom and Dad as I continued to walk the trail.

My parents were a great team in life, one completing the other, one strong where the other was weak, one wise where the other struggled, one serious where the other saw the humor, each devoted to the other – and both devoted to all of us. They were married for 57 years when my mother, not three weeks after their wedding anniversary of October 22, drifted out of her mortal restraints.

How is it that 57 years together, somehow, is still not enough time? How could 57 years be too short? How could my mother leave my father? Did she really leave, at all?

Do we all just drift through life, hopeful that we make it to shore, with the ones we love most?

I wondered if my journey would take me to my mother. Would I drift back to my mother, here and now, or is the memory of her enough for me to know she is always drifting with me, no matter where I am, or how far I walk. Maybe, with each step I take, she is drifting near me, riding the breeze that gently passes over my shoulders, the breeze that moves my hair just a little, the breeze that is moving in the direction the trail leads.

Maybe I don't need to imagine, or hope, to be with my mother on this mystical trail.

I'm already doing it.

Experience

Am I going to be on this trail forever? It felt as though I spoke with Grandmom Philly a lifetime ago.

The trail now widened, opening beautifully and, though I could not see the ocean from where I was, I could hear surf and seagulls. The rhythmic smashes of the ocean waves as they met the rocky Maine shoreline. I could almost picture each wave, brilliantly soaked in shimmering sunlight, pouring onto the mix of jagged and smoothed rock edges waiting for them on land. Acadia National Park stretches for miles of coastal beauty, no stranger to the gently flowing, sometimes roaringly spectacular watery hills and valleys bordering most of its existence.

I must be near Sand Beach. A bend in the trail ahead gave me hope that I would soon set eyes on the ocean.

Sand Beach is a little piece of heaven nestled between Acadia National Park's mountains and rocky shores on the east side of the region's Mount Desert Island. Access is only by way of Park Loop Road, just south of Bar Harbor. Of course, you can set foot on Sand Beach by taking any one of several wooded trails, just like this one – navigating your way through trees until you see one of Maine's most beautiful sand and shell beaches.

How many waves did my children and I splash in at Sand Beach over the summers? How many tiny footprints of my children dotted the sands of Sand Beach as, summer after summer until my children were no longer children, we enjoyed the pounding surf, little toes dipping in just enough to feel the energy of the Atlantic Ocean. Summer after summer, a million forgotten breaths and blinks ago, Sand

Beach was the canvas on which my young family painted some of its most beautiful memories, caressed by waves that traveled the Atlantic all the way to us.

I could hear the ocean even louder now.

Keeping a healthy pace, with the sun leading me step by step, I began to feel a crisp coolness surround me, almost like water. The push of my hands against the air felt more like pushing ripples against a tiny lake current than moving air. I was in water, but I was not in water. I was walking but weightless. My knees and hips seemed to lift above the dirt just enough to allow me to keep my stride a pebble's distance above the Earth itself.

At one point I stopped walking entirely, just to see if I would continue to float forward with no motion from me whatsoever. When I stopped moving, my feet planted themselves firmly back on top of the soil, and I stood there, in the silence of the sunbeams, wondering what had just happened.

"Oh, so you noticed *that*, did you?" a woman's voice called out to me.

Did she have an English accent?

Who did I know with an English accent?

No one.

"Well, you can't be standing there just waiting for something to happen, like a pickle in a barrel. Unless you think you a pickle in a barrel, you look betwixt, but I can see you ain't a calf lolly, not at all, refined is that I would say, refined and, prithee, a touch nice you feel to me," the woman said, appearing now out of the air.

She stood a few feet from me. I had no idea who this woman could possibly be, except she must have some connection to me or else, why is she here? Then again, I barely understood what I was doing here. Maybe I'm the one out of place? Maybe I am part of *her* experience?

"We kindred, ya *dizzy*," the woman said, laughing a bit, eyebrows meeting in a peak.

She looked at me as you do a lost puppy. Her face, calm and knowing, I sensed a patience in her and, as she paced closer to me, I felt an odd familiarity.

"Ay, then, you are a gentle one, I see good faith within, good faith."

I began to feel as though I was standing in water again.

Motionless, I just looked at the woman, who took in a deep breath for her next installment.

"You a bit buxom, no doubt many a man took a shine, that's good. We are of a long, long, long line of beauties I tell you," she uttered, as she brushed a hand over the whisps of her hair that blew around her eyes and, with the other hand, pulled her skirt a bit to tighten over her hip.

She must have sensed my absolute confusion. Her next words took me a minute to decipher, but I got her gist.

"Worry not, this is no Banbury Story, not at all, this is all very real, ridiculous, and absolutely, I promise, absolutely real. I'm sorry I cannot offer you a nipperkin, that might make all this easier, but here we are anyway, together in bedlam, far from King and Country."

Far from King?

What King?

I thought of my mother.

In the years before she left me, in her retirement that was cut entirely too short, she became an avid ancestry investigator. Hours and hours she would spend researching my father's lineage digging back generations to Greece and Italy's most southern villages. In her line, she dove hundreds of years deep in English and Irish heritage, taking us all with her to before the age of Robert the Bruce, who, she was certain, was a distant relative on her mother's side.

The woman took my hand, abruptly, but with a gentleness, and a hint of ownership.

"Let's walk a bit together, I only have you for a little bit, but I wanted to get a look at you," she said to me, giving her long skirt a snap to the right, kicking out a black boot from beneath as she adjusted her frock. It was only then that I noticed her clothing was meticulously lined, as if freshly adorned.

Not of this time, yet new.

"Life Is not always what you think it is, is it child?" she asked me. "Sometimes, you think one thing, you are sure as rain that you know it all, and then you see it in a new way, you feel life in a new way, and what you thought was up, is down. What you swore was air is water," she told me, with an almost loving tone. "That's the kind of day this is, it's a day that is not a day at all."

That's when I realized who she was, and I wasn't sure if she gave me this thought, or somewhere, somehow, my mother's years of sharing her ancestry investigations inspired me to remember, but, suddenly, and to my surprise, I knew exactly who I was walking with right now.

"Are you ... *Experience*?"

The woman stopped walking, bumped up against me, and started walking again.

"Yes, I knew you would understand," she said, with the pride of motherly acknowledgement.

Thanks to my mother, and all of her diligent ancestry investigations, I knew that my seventh great grandfather, on my mother's maternal side, was a man named John French who was born on April 16, 1699, in Braintree, Massachusetts, his father was Robert, and his mother, Experience. Robert and Experience had arrived in Massachusetts, from Thornbury, Gloucestershire, England, in May of 1691. Experience lived until the age of 64, when she died in in her own bed, in her Massachusetts home, far from the cobblestone streets of Thornbury where she ran as a girl, an ocean away from the farmlands that grew her bones.

Experience finished out her life millions and millions of ocean waves and ripples from the Gloucestershire origins of her birth, the very bit of land that enchanted Henry VIII and Anne Boleyn for a few days of romance more than a century before Experience took her first breath.

I had no idea how I remembered any of that, but I did.

And Experience could see that I did.

And somewhere, somehow, I knew that my mother was amused.

"Well, 'tis time," she said, as she stopped our pace.

Standing together, we were very still. I could no longer hear the sounds of ocean waves crashing in the distance. Only the inquisitive chirping of birds, and busily scurrying patters of woodland creatures.

Experience smiled at me, and as she gently released my arm from hers, I could see she was beginning to float, at first almost imperceivable, but within a few seconds it was clear she was rising up, moving her hands at her sides playfully, as if gently making waves in a lake, her long skirt moving with an unseen current that was gently carrying Experience away as the tips of her black boots gave away the playful kicking of her feet, as if swimming. As she continued to drift up, she smiled at me and gave me a knowing look, immediately I thought of the strength and endurance Experience must have had in her lifetime. Leaving the land of her birth, journeying an ocean, in the hopes the waves would lift and carry her dreams to fulfillment in a strange new land. Did she ever see her parents again? Did she ever feel truly at home, away from home?

Did Experience ever feel alone?

Did she ever walk with her own everyones?

Am I one of her ... everyones?

I knew not one answer to any of the questions popping into my mind as I watched Experience smoothly transition from form to figment. Still, I realized that her being part of this experience, for me, was intentional. She journeyed, once again, to touch something unfamiliar, in the hopes of supporting, maybe even creating, a dream. She rode waves, once again, waves now invisible, but tangible, to leave her mark, not on a new world, but on a tired soul – one connected to her through time.

What a remarkably strong woman Experience must have been, to be so brave. What a remarkably kind woman Experience must *still* be, to take on another journey.

"It's good to know you, Experience," I called out, as the faintest lines of her form were beginning to flow away into golden ripples of sunlight. "You must have been remarkable!"

She laughed, and with her laugh I could once again here the ocean meet the sand.

"Aren't we all remarkable? Isn't all this remarkable? Don't you want to see more, years and years and years more?" Experience said, returning my smile with her own. "You … walk your journey. Put any fears you have aside, child, any heart pains, any fallen dreams, any fright of illness, you must … remain. Stay strong, for family, for all of us. Pray, remember me. And pray, remember yourself too – and all you have still to do."

Her final words were practically whispers in the air, floating on unseen currents. I watched as Experience drifted up on the invisible waves that gently carried her perhaps back to her Massachusetts home, or to the Thornbury cobblestones of her youth, or, perhaps even to my mother, her great, great, great, great, and then some great granddaughter, maybe waiting for her, somewhere in the tapestry of twigs and time that exist in this experience beyond belief.

Experience…thank you.

I realized, if not for her, I would have never experienced a thing in this lifetime. I would never have existed. My mother would never have existed. My mother's mother would never have existed. Generations of mothers and fathers, daughters and sons, aunts and uncles, nieces, and nephews, would never have existed in my family. A woman I did not know, could not know, and would never have known existed at all, had it not been for the painstakingly thorough research of my mother.

A woman lost to time – *almost*.

Experience lived her life.

My mother lived her life.

I am living my life.

We are all connected, and, in the waves of twigs and time that fortify this trail, we so remain.

About Time

As I continued my pace, walking with each step into a clearing, I noticed, at first just a few, then many dozens of golden rose petals lining the trail, building in numbers on the dirt.

As I took a step, more seemed to drift into place, or appear from the ground itself, turning the trail golden in some patches with the volume of petals collecting. The petals were so abundant that they began to layer on themselves in increased spots. I couldn't see the golden petals falling to the ground anymore, they just seemed to appear.

Beautiful and full, like rose petals dipped in gold, shimmering in the sun.

I could see the layers of petals creating a golden trail, decorating the clearing with swirls of sparkling gold dotting over the dirt, grass, and twigs. The more I walked, the more the path of golden petals formed, one petal after the next, shimmering with the brightness of dozens, maybe hundreds, maybe thousands of intricately etched little suns.

I followed this brilliant trail of radiant petals, all the way to the one person I thought would have shown himself sooner. His shoulders in the distance, illuminated by the shimmer of falling golden rose petals, carved a figure into the clearing.

My husband.

Standing on the golden petals, he waited for me. When he left us all, without warning, and not that long ago, it cracked me. Broken cracks all through me, cracks that cannot be seen, cracks that never heal. He smiled at me and reached out his hand, which met my own, already reaching out for him.

"About time, took you long enough," my husband said to me. "I've been standing here all day."

I laughed.

I had no words.

I had too many words.

We hugged, and he kissed me with the newness of a first kiss and the longing of forever. As we kissed, my backpack fell to the ground, causing the layers of golden petals collecting at our feet to rise in the air, and surround us on a gust of sweet August air that breathed over us. The golden petals brushed against my cheeks as my husband and I gave in to the magic of the impossible. When I opened my eyes, and we put the hot August air between our mouths, I could see that he was wearing a tuxedo, and I was in my wedding gown. Our bodies pressing against one another, as if each were only standing thanks to the support of the other, we found ourselves meticulously presented, the delicate lines of my white gown against the stark black of his suit.

We were as we were on our wedding day.

Young.

Beautiful.

Healthy.

Golden.

"Remember how I lost my wedding ring in the hole in my tux pants right after the ceremony?" he laughed. "I thought we were done right then!"

"Funny, that was ridiculous, right, and yes, you were almost done right then!" I said to him, realizing the hands I placed around his shoulders and neck were now very youthful, and my hair, no longer reflecting the walk of my day, was rich and radiant, falling around my shoulders in voluminous waves of chestnut and auburn, the strands picking up the sunlight that embraced us.

My husband and I, standing together, were as we were on our wedding day. His hands around my waist were familiar and missed. His lips on mine, a memory revisited. As he kissed me, I could feel the golden petals all around us, the dipped on bold blooms of roses that led me here, rise up again, and surround our faces, forming, for me, a bridal veil that, as each golden petal pushed against the next, cascaded around my cheeks, framing my face, and flowing to the ground. The veil of what was embodied of some kind of magical tulle and lace secured to my head. The breeze continued to adorn us as our radiance shocked even us.

I could see the golden hues of light in my husband's eyes, his brown eyes looking golden, unnaturally enriched with a deepened resplendency that caused his eyes to shimmer.

Is any of this happening?

My husband looked at me with amusement.

"You don't believe any of this, do you?" he asked.

His smile grew massive.

"Yes, I do," I replied, knowing there was very little that would surprise me at this point.

He kissed my forehead.

Then, he kissed the tip of my nose.

"Well, I'm glad to believe in this because it's as real as you and I were and as real as you still are," my husband said, taking my lips with his own. I closed my eyes. This moment was everything. His warm hands on my waist, his mouth into mine, his energy pouring from him into me with a radiating warmth that seemed to heal all my weaknesses, vanquishing any trace of logic or reason I had lingering within me.

This moment was real.

He was real.

I was real.

We held hands, completely at home in the sun sparkles that celebrated us.

"You know, this is everything," he told me.
"We *are* everything."

I closed my eyes.

I wanted to feel the moment, more than even see it, I wanted to feel every sparkle of gold.

"You know," my husband's voice caressed the air, as he held me close. "We can't stay like this, at least, not yet. It's too soon for you, but don't worry, we are everything, and we will be everything, when it is no longer too soon for you."

His voice sounded different, deeper, trembling, and older. Opening my eyes, I could see he was changing.

My husband was aging, aging beyond the age he was when he died not too long ago. In fact, decades older he appeared. Still in his tux, smiling at me, now through aged eyes, he kissed the wedding ring on my left hand. To my shock, my hand was now aged much older than my years too. We looked very much older, advanced in years, and yet, we felt stronger than ever. Still in our wedding attire, now fitting with wrinkles and pulls, I felt comfortable in my advanced state of being. I felt a calmness and tranquility, as if I had lived long enough to fully earn the beautifully significant wrinkles in my hands, fingers and, I was certain, neck, face and everywhere else. I felt tired, weakened, and utterly empowered. I felt foreign to worry and fear. I felt old enough to have earned my peace, my walk in the forever.

I felt free.

Almost too free.

I felt as if all I had to do was just let go, to allow my lungs to empty, to whisper to nothing and, with my final push of air, I would be sunlight itself, dancing in the air, enveloping all around me. It's remarkable how very little it would take, to be a part of forever.

"We're still pretty sexy, for old people," my husband joked.

Snapping me back to this impossible moment, I laughed.

He always knew when I was lost in my thoughts.

He always knew when I was lost.

We smiled at each other, two old people, standing together in golden beams of sunlight.

"You see sweetheart," his broken voice carried. "We did have it all, we had our lifetime."

As he kissed my hand again, the golden petals collecting at our feet were raised up by a summery rush of air that caressed us, filling the air with gold bursts as sunlight danced over each gently floating petal. As my husband kissed my hand, I could see he, too, began to move into the August breeze, with sparks of gold popping from the corsage on his tuxedo, spellbindingly shimmering around the both of us, until I could see we were each the age we were when I first encountered him in the mythical clearing.

"I love you," he said. "Tell the kids I love them, and, when you are ready, I'm here waiting for you, but that's going to be many years from right now – *just so you know*."

He winked, his aged, wrinkled face gleefully hiding some great secret. As he brought my right palm up to his mouth to kiss, the feel of his lips and the warmth of his face seemed almost feverish. Kissing my palm, resting his face in my hand as we stood, leaning into one another, he began to fade gently and serenely into the hot August air, until all that was before me were golden petals, rising and falling around me, just me, as they hovered into the air, gently breaking apart, flowing into the breeze, until each petal fused with the air and joined the forever.

Just like my husband.

Alone in the clearing, the brilliant indigo sky above me, I opened my palm to see one perfect golden petal. I held it to my cheek, feeling the softness of the petal against my skin.

"We *did* have a lifetime," I spoke to the air, to my husband, to the forever.

For a moment, I felt a supernatural stillness.

The insignificance of my body in the middle of all this wonder. The joy in the empty. The echo in the silence. The connectedness of everything, of me, of *everyone*. I felt taken by the forever. The air surrounding me, the crispness of the day filling the space between me and the dirt, me and the sky, me and the forever that was living all around me in the unseen, yet experienced.

The forever that brought my husband to me, young and old, then gone, yet here still somehow in the softness of the air caressing my cheeks. The forever that brought me from Mifflin Street to Upland, from the laughter of my cousin to the enduring love guiding me forward, the love of an eternity of journeys all dissecting with my own. My grandfathers. My grandmothers. My mother. The familiar entities of light, timeless and ever present around me, within me and of me.

The forever of the trail, decorated with the gleam of a million blessed rose petals. This was a forever moment, happening during a forever day.

Maybe I was forever.

"You are ready now," a familiar voice called out to me.

Opening my eyes, I saw him.

Grandpop Tony.

My Last Walk

Walking with Grandpop Tony again was a very welcome experience. I had hoped I would get more time with him before whatever this experience was ended. Side by side, from the clearing, we walked down a narrow path, just enough room for us to touch shoulders as we kept a slow pace together, walking with purpose, but in no particular hurry.

"How are you feeling," Grandpop Tony asked.

I let the sound of my footsteps grinding against the dirt of the trail organize my thoughts.

"You know," I said to my grandfather. "I feel really good, Grandpop. I feel really good."

"I'm glad, we are always with you, you don't have to be afraid of anything, and you don't have to go through anything alone – not ever," Grandpop Tony told me, leaning in a little so that his shoulder bumped gently against mine. "I know sometimes, sometimes it feels like there is nothing but problems, life can do that sometimes. Life tests us. Whether you're dying, or fighting to live, or worrying about someone who is dying or fighting to live, whatever it is, life tests us. The thing is, Penny, what you always need to remember is that life, tests and all, is always, always worth living – and you never know what tomorrow may bring."

I reached out for his hand because I could sense this was goodbye. I noticed the gravel beginning to spark with golden pops and bursts under Grandpop Tony and, looking further down the trail we were navigating together, I could see actual people.

Regular people.

Normal people.

People.

"I love you Grandpop," I told him, squeezing his hand.

"I know you do," he told me, as he stopped walking, moving his hand forward as it was still in mine. "Now, I want you to go on, don't look back, and get something to eat and rest. It's been a long day, and I know you have a lot to think about and, I hope, a lot to be thankful for too."

The more we stood together, still holding hands, the golden pops and bursts around Grandpop Tony grew in numbers until the vibrancy of the golden shimmers danced off the lenses of his glasses, casting sunlight all around his head and mine.

"The sunbeams are calling you, aren't they," I said to him.

"Well, actually it's your grandmother calling me, and you know the mouth on her," he laughed.

He always spit a little when he laughed.

"Funny," I said to him, smiling, leaning into him. "And true!"

With that, I let his hand go.

We held one another in a gaze of goodbye for a few seconds before I turned away from him to do what he had instructed. The more I walked, the wider the trail grew, and I could hear the sounds of music, people in conversation, the rolling crunch of bikes on dirt and gravel. I stopped, just before I emerged off of the solitary trail I traveled.

I did what Grandpop Tony told me not to do.

I turned around.

There they all were.

Everyone.

It was a timeless sea of faces, and loving smiles. It was overwhelming, the silhouettes, shadows and fully formed people assembled to see me off, to wish me well. All gathered in this one space and time, to remind me I was loved, and would always be loved, always connected and, in the connection, always be a part of the forever.

There she was ... my favorite.

My beautiful mother, standing next to her beloved sister, my warm and loving Aunt Marie. My mother's face was the last face I focused on, her smile and strength transferring to me. Her hair gently danced around her face. Her cheeks, flush with color. Her green eyes, almost sparkling. Everything about her, strong and healthy, standing almost directly in line with me, she smiled, her high cheek bones forming the loveliest lines around her porcelain face. Raising her eyebrows and motioning her chin up slightly, encouraging me to go. I held up my right hand, put it to my heart, and closed my eyes.

I could feel the tears, tears of joy and love, tears of memories packed deep away, rush over my cheeks. I didn't want to open my eyes right away, because as the tears came, I knew they would wash me away from this sacred moment.

It was over, this walk of my lifetime, this walk with everyone. I opened my eyes. They were gone. I was alone, yet I could still feel their energy still with me.

I could still feel the strength of my mother, motioning me forward. Her stoic beauty and sublime gesture, just a little chin lift, a reassuring smile, leading me to pause, gather myself, and, without panic or fear, without hesitation, simply drift forward, drift on the waves of my journey, drift toward my shore.

Feeling as if on a wave in the ocean, the weightless support of millions upon millions of molecules keeping me buoyant, gently carrying me forward, until my feet were planted firmly on the damp soil of the now thickly settled wooded trail. Tones of people talking, bike treads crunching thick soil and an abundance of very active birds chirping filled the space around me. I heard a baby crying in the distance and the faint barking of a dog – not my Sammie, but one of this space and time. I searched the ground around my feet for paw prints, wondering if Sammie traveled with me back to the here and now.

There were no fresh paw prints encircling me, but I did hear the faintest ring of ting, ting, tinging drifting from the thickness of bush and trees from which I had drifted.

Secure on my feet, and enlivened by my walk with everyone, I took my first slow steps on the busy trail. I didn't recognize anyone around me.

Not one familiar face, nor hint of a sunbeam.

Not a single smile in my direction, or brush with any remote acquaintances. I was surrounded by people, flesh, and bone people, but utterly and poetically alone.

I took a deep breath, filling my lungs with the earthy dampness that was the air around me.

I did not feel alone.

I would never feel alone again.

Today

When I got back to our beloved Maine cabin, all my children were there. Thank goodness my son remembered where we always hid the spare rental key. I wasn't expecting them all until much later into the evening, so when I pulled up and saw my son and his family, my daughters and some of their friends had arrived, I was overjoyed.

After settling in for a dinner of fresh tossed salad loaded with ripe tomatoes, cucumber, red onions and carrots, baked macaroni-and-cheese, and more fish sticks than we could eat, we settled in for a long night of storytelling around the firepit, the echoing sounds coming off the water blanketing us all. The kids baked me a birthday cake, which was more chocolate than I could handle, but I loved it.

We talked about their drives up, what's new in their lives and I told stories of my Grandpop Tony. Everyone always loves the one about the Ford Galaxie. We talked about how much we missed their Dad, and we laughed about the time he tipped his kayak over in the lake, splashing and yelling like a lunatic in three feet of water. We laughed about the old story of how my Pop Pop went hunting alone in the woods one time, stopped for lunch by a tree, and woke up in the dark of night after falling asleep.

We shared memories of Maine vacations through the years, our explorations together across the majestic cliffsides of Acadia National Park. We texted my father, sharing pictures of our firepit assembly, wishing he was here with us so that he could break everyone up with his stories about his crazy uncles. After more stories than most of the family could stay awake to hear, we nestled into our beds and bunks for the night. The next morning, the sun came up, and it was glorious. It was a new day.

Today…it was a new today.

Yesterday, I was spectral, gifted with so much love and care. It was the greatest day of my life, the greatest birthday of my life. It was the greatest first day of the rest of my life.

Yesterday I was reminded I am a stitch in the tapestry of my family, connected through time forever to those who cared for me, and cared for those who would someday care for me.

Yesterday, I was renewed, encouraged to live my life one day after the next, with faith and belief in the magical, belief in the forever.

And that is exactly what I am going to do.

Today, we are all going to Acadia National Park to walk the trails together, and see some of our favorite sights, especially Bubble Pond. My body feels good. My soul feels good. What's more, I got a voicemail this morning from my doctor's office, informing me that my most recent test results are looking great, far better than could be hoped for, and for me to stay the course.

Today is going to be a beautiful and busy day. I can feel it. I think tonight, after we settle back in from our adventures, I'll make celery things. My Mom would like that – I am sure of it.

23 Years Later

All I could think about was how she looked, the wind circling her, the smooth sunbeams tracing every line of her as she walked toward me. You can see the wind, you know, when you are a part of it. It's blue and yellow, sometimes it looks like sparkles.

The wind was never invisible, it was never just the movement of leaves on a tree or the pushing of your hair, or body. It was always this visible, beautiful, alive thing – it was always there, I just couldn't see it before I died.

Once I died, I could see the wind.

I could see everything.

I saw my father. He took me on a walk to his birthplace in Isle of Pines, as it was known in his boyhood, in his own father's lifetime. A Cuban paradise, the remote wonder that is Isla de la Juventud, just about 60 or so miles south of mainland Cuba. A pirate cove. A forgotten island rich in spices and the ghosts of buried treasures. It was on the sands of Isle of Pines that my father told me I was starting a new time of my existence.

The hardest part about being dead is being dead. Once you get used to it, though, you can see the positives. No more pain. No more sadness. You miss your life, your people, your love, but you don't really miss anything else, because you have everything else.

When I saw her on her walk, it was the best day of my existence.

Stumbling a bit with the canopy of pedals and sunbeams swirling around her, she made her way cautiously to me. She didn't know I had been walking with her almost her entire time. I was sometimes behind her, marveling at how she was soaking in the unbelievable. At times, I was paces ahead of her, excited to get her to the place where she would be in my arms again. I won't go into how I left her, and our kids, because this isn't really my story.

It's hers.

I guess my time was just up, we can leave it at that because, in the end, that's really what happened. My time was just up. Seeing her, though, on her walk, with her family guiding her, I was so proud of her. Pushing through all the crap of her cancer, trying to keep strong for our kids and still, even with how she must have felt most of the time, still willing herself to see her glass as half full – to be thankful for the glass at all.

That was my wife.

That is my wife.

It was 23 years ago today that I saw her again.

A moment.

Our lifetime.

Now, I'm standing in the same spot. I cannot wait. That may sound selfish of me, I know. I can be a real asshole sometimes, I guess. Selfish or not, I cannot wait until she is here, with me. From the first day I saw her, I knew she was my home. Boy, was she hot. All the flowing hair, thick brown curls everywhere. Her eyes. Her smile.

Just her.

I cannot wait to see her again. It was too short last time, but it was as long as she needed it to be then, just long enough for her to know I am with her, she is loved, and she had a lot more living to do. When I held her, and the wind covered us, I could feel she had so much more life to do. I knew I could not keep her with me. That power is not mine. I could only be thankful to have her with me again. To be able to be a part of her journey on that day, the most important walk of her lifetime.

It was 23 years ago today that I saw her again.

Today is the day she comes back to me.

Today is the day I can show her everything, even the sands of Isla de la Juventud. Today is our day to begin our new existence *together*, in the sunbeams and sands of forever.

I cannot wait to walk with her.

Printed in Great Britain
by Amazon